P9-DFF-351

Before he could talk himself out of it, Lucas reached out and pulled her into his arms.

"I'm just so scared," she admitted. "Not for me but for Camden and you. For your family."

"No one is going to hurt Camden or my family," he assured her. Not that he was in a position to give that kind of assurance. Not with hired guns after them. Still, those hired guns would have to get past him, and since he was protecting his son, Lucas had no intentions of making that easy for them.

Hailey looked up at him at the exact moment he looked down at her. He was so not ready for this. Well, his mind and heart weren't anyway, but the rest of him seemed to think it was a good idea to kiss her or something.

Especially something.

The heat came. Memories, too. Vivid memories of Hailey naked and beneath him in his bed.

The very bed that was just up the hall.

LUCAS

USA TODAY Bestselling Author

DELORES FOSSEN

If you purchased this book without a cover you should be aware that this book is stolen property. It was reported as "unsold and destroyed" to the publisher, and neither the author nor the publisher has received any payment for this "stripped book."

Recycling programs
for this product may
not exist in your area.

ISBN-13: 978-0-373-75673-5

Lucas

Copyright © 2017 by Delores Fossen

All rights reserved. Except for use in any review, the reproduction or utilization of this work in whole or in part in any form by any electronic, mechanical or other means, now known or hereinafter invented, including xerography, photocopying and recording, or in any information storage or retrieval system, is forbidden without the written permission of the publisher, Harlequin Enterprises Limited, 225 Duncan Mill Road, Don Mills, Ontario M3B 3K9, Canada.

This is a work of fiction. Names, characters, places and incidents are either the product of the author's imagination or are used fictitiously, and any resemblance to actual persons, living or dead, business establishments, events or locales is entirely coincidental.

This edition published by arrangement with Harlequin Books S.A.

For questions and comments about the quality of this book, please contact us at CustomerService@Harlequin.com.

® and TM are trademarks of Harlequin Enterprises Limited or its corporate affiliates. Trademarks indicated with ® are registered in the United States Patent and Trademark Office, the Canadian Intellectual Property Office and in other countries.

HARLEQUIN®
™ www.Harlequin.com

Printed in U.S.A.

Delores Fossen, a *USA TODAY* bestselling author, has sold over fifty novels with millions of copies of her books in print worldwide. She's received a Booksellers' Best Award and an RT Reviewers' Choice Best Book Award. She was also a finalist for a prestigious RITA® Award. You can contact the author through her website at www.deloresfossen.com.

Books by Delores Fossen

Harlequin Intrigue

The Lawmen of Silver Creek Ranch

Grayson
Dade
Nate
Kade
Gage
Mason
Josh
Sawyer
Landon
Holden
Drury
Lucas

HQN Books

A Wrangler's Creek Novel

Lone Star Cowboy (ebook novella)
Those Texas Nights
One Good Cowboy (ebook novella)
No Getting Over a Cowboy

Visit the Author Profile page at Harlequin.com for more titles.

CAST OF CHARACTERS

Lucas Ryland—A Texas Ranger who'll do anything to protect his infant son. That includes protecting his ex, Hailey Darrow, even if he's never forgiven Hailey for walking out on him.

Hailey Darrow—She's been in a coma for three months, but awakes to find she's given birth to a son and there's a killer after her.

Camden Ryland—Lucas and Hailey's son. Someone is trying to kidnap him to get to Hailey.

Eric DeSalvo—A powerful businessman with criminal ties. He's worried that Hailey might have information that could send him to prison.

Preston DeSalvo—Hailey helped send this late tycoon to jail, but someone could want to avenge his death by silencing Hailey for good.

Brian Minton—An FBI agent who might have been on Preston DeSalvo's payroll. Is he the one who wants Hailey dead?

Colleen Jeffrey—Hailey's half sister. She has secrets that could put Lucas, Hailey and their son in danger.

Chapter One

Texas Ranger Lucas Ryland stared at the bed in the room at the Silver Creek Hospital.

It was empty.

He touched his fingers to the sterile white covers, already knowing they wouldn't be warm. According to the doctor, no one had been in that bed for at least the last fifteen minutes.

Maybe longer.

Mumbling something that Lucas didn't catch, Dr. Alfred Parton paced across the room. The doctor had already told Lucas that he wasn't sure how long the *patient* had been missing. That was one of the first things he had told Lucas when he called him. Of course, first Dr. Parton had dropped the bombshell.

Hailey Darrow is gone.

Lucas had rushed to the hospital to see for himself. And now that he had seen the empty bed with his own eyes, it didn't help with the jolt of adrenaline he'd gotten.

"How the hell did this happen?" Lucas demanded.

"No idea." Dr. Alfred Parton scrubbed his hand over his balding head, something he'd been doing a lot since Lucas had arrived. "I've asked everyone on the staff, and no one knows. But Hailey must have had some help. She wouldn't have been able to get up and just walk out of here."

No. Not after being in a coma for three months. She wouldn't have been able to stand on her own, much less get out of the bed and leave the building.

Of course, that only brought on a boatload of questions for Lucas—had she awakened and managed to talk someone into helping her leave? It was a valid concern, because the last time Lucas had seen Hailey conscious, she'd been nine months pregnant with their child and running. Not just from some guy who'd been chasing her.

But also running from him.

He'd found her, finally, unconscious from a car accident. She'd plowed into a tree, and a limb that'd come through the windshield had given her a nasty head injury. She'd also had a fake ID and enough cash for Lucas to know that she had planned on disappearing.

Even now, three months later, that felt like a punch to the gut, but a "punched gut" feeling pretty much described his entire relationship with Hailey for the year he'd known her.

"We have some security cameras," the doctor explained, "but none back here in this part of the hospital. They're at the front entrance, the ER and the pharmacy. We're still looking, but she's not on any of that footage."

Which meant she might still be inside the place. It wasn't a huge hospital, but there were clinics, storage closets and probably some un-occupied rooms.

"You think she'll try to go to the Silver Creek Ranch?" the doc asked.

Lucas cursed and yanked out his phone. He'd been so shocked by the news that Hailey was missing that he hadn't even considered the next step of how this might play out.

But, yeah, if she was capable of moving, she would almost certainly try to get to his cousins' ranch, where Lucas now lived. Hailey would try to get to the baby.

Camden.

His three-month-old son.

But he was Hailey's child, too.

And Hailey would go after him. Or rather,

she would try. As far as Lucas was concerned, Hailey had given up her rights to their precious little boy when she'd gone on the run before Camden was born. Hailey had endangered herself and the baby in that car wreck.

"Search every inch of the hospital," Lucas ordered the doctor, though that was just the frustration talking because the staff was already looking for Hailey. "And let me know the second you find her."

Lucas headed out the door, hurrying, but he didn't call Camden's nanny because he didn't want to alarm her, yet. Instead, he called his cousin, Mason Ryland. Mason was a part-time deputy in Silver Creek, but since it was nearly 8:00 p.m., he'd already be home, and his house was just up the road from Lucas's new place.

"I'm not coming into the office," Mason said instead of a greeting. His cousin wasn't the friendliest of the Ryland clan, but he would protect Camden with his life.

Lucas prayed it didn't come down to that, though.

"Hailey's missing from the hospital," Lucas tossed out there. "I'm on my way home now, but make sure she doesn't get anywhere near Camden."

Mason cursed, too, and it was ripe enough

that Lucas heard Mason's wife, Abbie, give him a scolding about saying such things in front of their two young sons.

"You can explain when you get here," Mason said. "I'll head over to your place now."

Lucas thanked him and hoped he did indeed have something to explain—like Hailey's whereabouts and how she'd managed to escape. Right now, he didn't know nearly enough.

He ran out of the building and across the parking lot to his SUV. The November wind swiped at him, but he didn't duck his head against it. Lucas kept watch around him. A habit that had saved him a time or two while he'd been a Texas Ranger. But nothing seemed out of the ordinary.

The moment he was behind the wheel, Lucas started the engine. However, before he could throw the SUV into gear, he caught the movement from the backseat. Lucas whirled around, already reaching for his gun.

But it was too late.

Hailey was there.

She was sitting right next to the baby's empty car seat, and thanks to the security lights, he could see that she had a gun pointed right at him. *His* gun. The one he kept as a backup in the glove compartment. Since he hadn't seen her when he first approached the vehicle, it likely meant she'd ducked down out of sight. Hiding from him so she could—well—do whatever the heck she was doing.

"Leave your weapon in your holster," she ordered, and it was indeed an order.

That was a hard look Hailey gave him. But the hardness didn't mesh well with the beads of sweat on her forehead. It was chilly, definitely not warm enough weather for sweating, so this must have been from exertion. There was no color in her cheeks. She looked weak, and no doubt was, but she didn't need much strength considering the gun she had in his face.

Lucas had no idea if she'd actually shoot him, because she clearly wasn't thinking straight. Couldn't be. Or else she wouldn't have him at gunpoint. Then again, she had run from him three months ago, so it was obvious she hadn't trusted him.

Still didn't, apparently.

The head injury that had put her in the coma had healed with the exception of a thin scar near her scalp. Her blond hair was pushed back from her face now so the scar was easier to see, but in another month or two, it'd be practically gone. No signs of the trauma that had nearly killed her and the baby.

No visible signs, anyway.

Lucas would always remember. *Always.*

"Start driving," Hailey insisted. "We can't stay here."

Because the hospital staff would look in the parking lot. But that didn't explain why she was hiding and clearly trying to escape.

Hell, it didn't explain a lot of things.

Lucas did drive. Not far, though, and only after he hit the child safety button to lock all the doors so that Hailey wouldn't be able to get out. He drove out of the parking lot and went two blocks up before pulling over.

He purposely didn't choose a spot in front of any businesses in case something went wrong when he wrestled that gun away from her. Instead, he stopped in front of the town park. Since it was already dark, the park was empty.

"All right. Now talk." Lucas had a string of questions but went with the easiest one first. "How'd you get from your room to my SUV?"

"I walked."

"Impossible," Lucas fired back. He glanced around to make sure someone wasn't out there ready to help her with more than just getting out of that hospital bed. "People who've been in a coma for three months just don't get up and walk."

She nodded. Dragged in a thin breath. That's when he noticed she was shaking. "I've been out of the coma for nearly a week now, and I've been exercising my legs when no one was watching."

Nearly a week.

Damn.

"And none of the medical staff noticed?" he snapped.

"I was never in a vegetative state, just a deep coma, so the monitor already showed plenty of brain activity for me. The activity increased when I woke up, but I tampered with the machine so that it looked as if it malfunctioned. I kept doing that, and the staff thought they had faulty readings."

A nurse had indeed told him about the readings, and the hospital had called in someone to repair the machine. The Silver Creek Hospital wasn't big or modern by anyone's standards so they hadn't had another monitor to use on Hailey. That's why the nurses had been keeping a closer watch on her. Obviously, they hadn't watched nearly close enough.

"How'd you know how to tamper with the monitor?" he pressed.

She glanced away. "I'm good with computers and such."

This was the first Lucas was hearing about

that, but it didn't matter. Not when there were so many other things they needed to talk about.

"When I was trying to regain my strength, I made sure no one else saw me," she added.

Obviously. Just as she'd made sure he hadn't noticed her before he'd gotten in his vehicle.

Her gaze dropped to her stomach for just a second. "I listened to try to find out if I'd had a boy or a girl, but no one mentioned it. Not even you when you visited me on Monday."

Clearly she'd known he was there. Lucas had indeed visited her, something he did a couple of times a week. Why, he didn't know, because he couldn't get answers from a woman in a coma. It riled him to the core, though, that she'd been awake during that visit and hadn't said anything.

But what had he said?

Lucas wasn't even sure—maybe nothing—but he'd almost certainly glared at her. He still was glaring now.

"So, you faked being in a coma for the last week, built up your strength, and just walked out of the hospital?" he asked, going through the probability of that as he said it.

He was skeptical.

Hailey nodded. "I ducked into a supply room, and when I heard the doctor call you, I knew you'd be arriving soon. I made my way to the parking lot and hid behind some shrubs."

"And then you broke into my SUV," Lucas snarled.

"The back door was unlocked," she answered as if that was something she did all the time. To the best of his knowledge, she didn't, but then, he really didn't know much about this woman.

The mother of his child.

"Why didn't you let me know you'd come out of the coma?" Lucas demanded.

Hailey stared at him a long time. "I'll tell you that if you'll tell me what I had—a boy or a girl?"

He debated bargaining with her. Even with that gun aimed at him. But it was probably best to give her the information so they could move on to something else. Something that involved his ripping that gun out of her hand.

"You had a boy," he finally said. "He was born three months ago."

"Three months?" she repeated. It sounded as if she had to choke back a sob. "That long."

Yeah, that long. "The doctors had to deliver him by C-section because you weren't conscious when you went into labor."

She shook her head, her breath shuddering. "I don't remember."

"Comas are like that," he said, and he didn't

bother to sound even marginally sympathetic. "I named him Camden David. But I have sole custody of him," Lucas added.

Not a lie, exactly. He did have custody of him and had tried to make it permanent, but the judge had refused on the grounds that Hailey might come out of the coma and her parental rights could be reinstated.

Could be.

Lucas would make sure that didn't happen.

Something went through her pale green eyes, and Hailey made a sound, part groan, part gasp. At first he thought maybe the reaction was due to his custody comment, but the tears proved otherwise. It was the reaction of a woman who'd just learned she had a son.

But she was a mother in name only.

"And he… Camden's all right?" Hailey asked, still blinking back those tears. "There were no problems with the delivery?"

"Yeah. No thanks to you."

"Is he safe?" she asked before Lucas could finish what he was about to say.

"Of course he is." Lucas couldn't stop himself from cursing. "What the hell were you thinking when you went on the run like that? And what happened to you? Were you driving too fast? Is that what caused the accident—and that?"

He pointed to her scar, but Lucas didn't pull

back his hand. He knocked the gun away from her, and it fell on the front passenger's seat. Hailey immediately scrambled to retrieve it, but Lucas was a whole lot faster. He dropped it on the floor, well out of her reach.

"Don't make me draw my gun," he warned her and took hold of her wrist in case she was about to try to get out the door.

But she didn't try to escape.

A hoarse sob tore from her mouth, and Hailey eased away from him. Just in case she had another weapon back there, Lucas leaned over the seat and did a quick check around her. He frisked her, too. Since she was wearing a pair of loose green scrubs, a thin sweater and flip-flops, there weren't many places she could conceal a weapon.

Still, after what'd happened three months ago, Lucas looked.

His hand brushed against the side of her breast, and she made a soft sound. Not the groan she'd made earlier. This one caused him to feel that tug deep within his body. But Lucas told that tug to take a hike.

Their gazes connected. Not for long. Lucas finished the search and found nothing.

"Now, keep talking," he insisted. "Tell me what happened to you. Why did you go on the run, and why didn't you tell anyone before now that you were out of the coma?"

She opened her mouth and got that deer-in-the-headlights look. What she didn't do was answer him.

"Enough of this," he mumbled.

He took out his phone to call Mason and then the sheriff, but as he'd done with her earlier, Hailey took hold of his hand. "Please don't tell your cousins. Not yet."

Since most of his Ryland cousins were cops, that wasn't what he wanted to hear. "Did you break the law? Is that why you were on the run?"

"No." She closed her eyes and shook her head. Her head wasn't the only thing shaking, though. She started to shiver, the cold and maybe the fear finally getting to her. "But I'm in trouble. God, Lucas, I'm in so much trouble."

He was about to curse at her for stating the obvious, but something else went through her eyes.

Fear.

"It won't take long for word to get out that I'm awake," Hailey said, speaking barely louder than a whisper. "And he'll find out."

"He?" Lucas snapped.

Hailey's voice cracked. "There's a killer after me."

Chapter Two

Hailey closed her eyes a moment, hoping it would help with the dizziness.

It didn't.

It was hard to think with her head spinning, the bone-deep exhaustion and the muscle spasms that kept rippling through her body.

Hard to think, too, with Lucas glaring at her as if she were the enemy. Of course, in his eyes, that's exactly what she was.

He obviously didn't believe her. Didn't trust her, either, but somehow Hailey had to make him understand. First, though, he had to take care of what was most important—the baby.

"Are you sure Camden is safe?" she asked.

That caused a new slash of anger to go through his eyes. Probably because he believed she was dodging the news she'd just dropped on him.

There's a killer after me.

"He's safe," Lucas finally said, but he spoke through clenched teeth. "Now, tell me why you need to make sure of that. Does it have something to do with the so-called killer?" He didn't give her a chance to say a word, though. "Or are you trying to lie your way out of why you ran from me three months ago?"

"It's not a lie." She wished it was. "But I didn't tell the truth about some other things."

That tightened the muscles in his jaw even more. "Start from the beginning, and so help me, there'd better not be any lies this time."

Hailey nodded but glanced around them. Since it was Tuesday and a school night, Silver Creek wasn't exactly teeming with activity, but she did spot someone jogging in the park. She kept her attention on him until he disappeared around the curve of the tree-lined trail. Maybe it was nothing. Maybe the guy was just that—a jogger—but he could have been someone after her.

"We need to find a better place to talk," Hailey told him.

Lucas gave her a flat look. Cursed. "I'm not taking you to the Silver Creek Ranch."

That was no doubt where the baby was.

Camden.

Hailey mentally repeated that, something she'd been doing since Lucas had first mentioned her precious son's name. Learning something—anything—about her baby caused her heart to ache. It felt as if someone was squeezing it hard.

Mercy, she'd lost so much already. Three months. And there was a lot more she could lose. Thank God the baby was okay, but it was up to her to make sure he stayed that way.

"I can't see Camden," Hailey answered. Saying it aloud added an even deeper pain. "Not until I'm sure it's safe."

"You won't see him at all," Lucas snapped. He spewed out more of that profanity. "You don't have a right to see him."

No, in his eyes, she didn't. But if and when this was over, she would see her son. Even if she had to push her way through an army of Ryland lawmen. No one would keep him from her.

Since it was obvious Lucas wasn't going to budge, Hailey tried to figure out the fastest way to convince him that it wasn't safe for her to be out in the open like this.

That meant starting from the beginning.

"I'm not who you think I am," she said.

A burst of air left his mouth, but it wasn't a laugh. "Obviously. You slept with me and then sneaked out, leaving me a note saying you couldn't see me again."

Hailey didn't need a reminder of that. She could have recited the note word for word.

Lucas, I'm sorry, but this was a mistake. I can't get involved with you.

"That was the truth," she continued. "I shouldn't have let things get so…intimate between us."

"But you did, and you got pregnant."

Yes, she had. Since they'd used a condom, the pregnancy definitely hadn't been something Hailey had been expecting. But that hadn't stopped her from wanting the child right from the start.

"Mistakes aside," Lucas continued, "you had no right to run away from me while you were carrying my baby." He cursed again. "If you hadn't had that car accident, I might have never found you. Of course, that was probably the plan, wasn't it? To run away so that I'd never be able to see my child?"

Hailey didn't even have to think about that answer. "No. That wasn't the plan."

He didn't believe her, but it was the truth.

"I was trying to stay alive, trying to keep the baby from being hurt," Hailey explained.

He tapped his badge. "I'm a Texas Ranger." That was probably his way of saying that if something was wrong, she should have gone straight to him.

But Lucas had been in danger, too.

Something he didn't know.

Yet.

Figuring she would need it, Hailey took another deep breath. "Two years ago, I was employed as a computer systems analyst in Phoenix for a man named Preston DeSalvo. I found out he was working with someone in the FBI. A dirty agent. And they were selling confiscated weapons. I went to the cops, DeSalvo was eventually arrested, and after I testified against him, I was placed in witness protection and given a new identity. The marshals relocated me here to Silver Creek."

She paused, giving him a few moments to let all of that sink in, but Lucas didn't take the time. He whipped out his phone again, and before she could stop him, she saw him press the contact for one of his cousins.

Sheriff Grayson Ryland.

"Don't tell him I'm with you," Hailey insisted. "The sheriff's office could be bugged."

She saw the debate Lucas was having with himself, but he didn't stop the call. He did put it on speaker, though, and it didn't take long before Grayson answered.

"I heard about Hailey," Grayson said right

off the bat. "I've sent two of the deputies to the hospital to help look for her."

"Thanks," Lucas said. And he paused. A long time. "Can you look up info on a guy named Preston DeSalvo?"

Grayson paused, too. Hailey knew the sheriff well because she'd worked for him as an emergency dispatcher shortly after her arrival in Silver Creek. Grayson had a lot of experience as a lawman and was probably suspicious.

"Is DeSalvo connected to Hailey?" Grayson asked, though she could hear the clicks of his computer keys.

"Maybe."

More keyboard clicking sounds. "Well, Preston DeSalvo was sent to prison about eighteen months ago. He's dead. Killed in a fight at a maximum security prison in Arizona a little over three months ago."

"Why was he in prison?" Lucas pressed.

"A laundry list of charges, including murder, extortion and gun running. An employee, Laura Arnett, testified against him, and she's in WITSEC." He huffed. "Now, what does this have to do with Hailey?"

"Maybe everything. I'll call you back when I know more. In the meantime, can you make sure the ranch is on lockdown?"

"Already have. Mason called and said you'd

asked him to go to your house. You think Hailey could be headed there?"

"I'll call you back," Lucas repeated, probably so that he wouldn't have to lie to his cousin.

But the stalling wouldn't last long. Soon, very soon, his cousins would be demanding answers. Especially Grayson, since he wasn't just the sheriff but also the head of the Ryland clan. However, Lucas would be demanding them first.

"Laura Arnett?" Lucas repeated. "That's your real name?"

She nodded. "I haven't thought of myself as that since all of this happened. I'm Hailey Darrow. For now, anyway. But I'll have to come up with another identity. DeSalvo's dead, but no one knows who his partner was," she added.

"The dirty FBI agent," he spat out like the profanity he tacked onto that. "And you believe he's after you?"

"I know he is. Well, one of his henchmen, anyway."

She glanced around again, praying that one of those thugs wasn't nearby, looking for her.

"I don't know how he found me," Hailey continued. "Maybe he hacked into the WITSEC files, or he could have bribed someone to give him the info. But three months ago, I found an eavesdropping device in my house here in Silver Creek, and I knew my identity had been blown."

"You should have come to me." His jaw muscles were at war with each other again. "Or since you were in WITSEC, you could have called your handler."

"I didn't get a chance. Before I could do anything, a hired gun showed up at my house. I hid, but he yelled out that if I didn't give myself up, he'd go after you and use you to get me to cooperate."

The skepticism was still written all over his face. "Cooperate with what?"

Oh, he was not going to like this. "I have some computer files that I didn't turn over to the cops. Files that incriminate Preston's son, Eric. Nothing as serious as murder, but it would have put him away for a few years."

"I'll want to see those files." And it wasn't a suggestion.

She nodded. "It'll take a while to access them. I put them in online storage with some security measures. I set it up so the files won't open until twelve hours after I put in the password."

"Clever," he mumbled, but Hailey didn't think that was a compliment. No. Lucas was silently cursing her for not bringing this to him sooner.

"I let Preston know I'd leak the files if anything happened to me," Hailey explained, "and that his son would head to prison right along with him. It was my insurance, a way of making sure he didn't send his hired thugs after me."

Lucas lifted his shoulder. "But he sent them anyway?"

"No. Preston was dead by then. I think the person who sent the thugs is the dirty agent. First, though, he wants those files."

"Or it could be his son who's after you," Lucas quickly pointed out.

"Maybe. But I didn't personally mention anything to Eric about having incriminating info on him."

Of course, that didn't mean Eric hadn't found out. Eric hadn't visited his father in prison. Not once. But Preston could have said something to one of his lackeys, who in turn passed the info on to Eric. Which wouldn't have necessarily been a bad thing. Because it could have kept Eric off her back, too, had he ever decided to come after her.

"How did you get away from that hired gun?" Lucas asked a moment later.

"I sneaked out the back of the house. I had a car, some cash and new identity papers in a storage unit." Hailey huffed. "I'll answer all your questions. I promise. But we can't stay here. In fact, you can't be with me."

He looked at her as if she'd just sprouted wings. "You think I'm going to dump you out here on the street?"

"No, but I was hoping you'd arrange to get me a car. Or let me use this SUV for a couple of hours."

"That's not going to happen. But I am taking you somewhere—to the sheriff's office."

"No." She couldn't say it fast enough, and Hailey went to the edge of her seat so she could take hold of his arm again. "Didn't you hear me? The office could be bugged. My hospital room was. That's why I didn't say anything to any of the medical staff. I wasn't sure who'd put it there or if I could trust any of them."

Lucas had already put the SUV in gear to drive away, no doubt to head toward the sheriff's office, but that piece of information stopped him. He turned, studying her, probably to decide how much of this was the truth.

Before he could make up his mind, his phone rang, and again she saw Grayson's name on the screen. She doubted Lucas would keep her secret much longer. He would spill everything to the sheriff.

And that meant she had to get out of there—fast.

But how? Lucas had all the doors locked,

and she wasn't nearly strong enough to break the windows.

"We might have a problem," Grayson said when Lucas answered, and he put the call on speaker. "Dr. Parton called, and he said right after you left, a man showed up looking for Hailey. He claimed he was her brother."

Oh, God. "I don't have a brother," she mouthed.

"Doc Parton got suspicious," Grayson went on. "And he just sent me the surveillance footage of the guy coming in through the ER entrance. I put his photo into the facial recognition program and got an immediate hit."

Lucas groaned, no doubt because he knew what that meant. If the guy was in the system, he had a record. "Who is he?" he asked the sheriff.

"Darrin Sandmire. A low-life thug." He paused. "Sandmire often works as a hit man."

Her heart slammed against her chest. It was happening. Her worst fears. The killer wasn't just after her. He was here in Silver Creek.

"Sandmire left the hospital before the security guard could stop him, so he could be anywhere in town. Now, you want to tell me what this is all about?" Grayson demanded.

"Yeah. I'll be at the sheriff's office in a few minutes." Lucas paused. "Hailey's with me."

The panic shot through her, and she tried the

door handle even though Hailey knew she was trapped. If Lucas took her to the sheriff's office, she might be putting not only herself in danger but also all of them. Lucas put the SUV in gear again, but something must have caught his eye, because his attention zoomed to the driver's side window.

To the park.

Hailey saw it then, as well. The jogger she'd spotted earlier. But this time, he wasn't on the trail. He was coming straight toward the SUV.

And he had a gun in his hand.

Chapter Three

"Get down!" Lucas shouted to Hailey.

His first instinct was to draw his gun and take aim at the man running toward them. But Lucas didn't want to get into a gunfight on Main Street where innocent bystanders—or Hailey—could be hurt.

Lucas wasn't sure he believed everything she'd just told him, but it was obvious she had someone after her. Later he'd find out who that was, but for now he wanted to put some distance between this armed man and them. He hit the accelerator.

Just as the guy took aim.

And fired.

The bullet slammed into the side of the SUV, missing the window and Lucas by only a couple of inches.

"I need a gun," Hailey said, climbing over the

seat to get to the passenger side. She started to fumble around for the weapon that he'd knocked away from her.

"Stay down," Lucas warned her, but her search took care of that. Hailey crawled onto the floor.

At least, it took care of it for a couple of seconds. Once she had the gun, she got back in the seat and took aim out the back side window.

She fired.

The sound blasted through the SUV, causing Lucas to curse. He hadn't actually expected her to shoot. Too bad she missed, because the gunman sent another bullet their way.

Lucas sped off. The thug got off one more shot before Lucas took the first turn he reached. He wasn't driving in the direction of the sheriff's office, but he could double back.

Lucas tossed Hailey his phone. "Call Grayson and tell him there's an armed man near the park at the intersection of Main and Everett Road."

Hailey made the call, but she kept watch behind them, making sure that goon wasn't in pursuit. The moment Grayson answered, she rattled off the information. Then she hit the end call button. No doubt because she didn't want to answer Grayson's questions. That was okay. For now.

But as soon as they reached the sheriff's office, Hailey had better come clean about everything.

Lucas took another turn. Then another, meandering his way back to Main Street. That particular part of the park was only about seven blocks away from the sheriff's office, so it wouldn't take Grayson long to get a pair of deputies there to catch the guy.

"Do you know if that was Darrin Sandmire?" Lucas asked her.

"I have no idea. But I'm pretty sure that was the same man who came after me three months ago."

Hell.

Lucas had to rein in the anger that sliced through him. That was the SOB who'd put Hailey—and therefore, Camden—in danger. Too bad Lucas hadn't managed to shoot him. But then he rethought that. He didn't want the guy dead, not until he had answers from him.

Like who hired him.

Thugs like Darrin Sandmire always worked for bigger thugs. Maybe DeSalvo's son, Eric. Maybe that unidentified rogue agent. Soon, Lucas intended to find out who'd paid this killer to come after Hailey.

Lucas took another turn, the tires squealing

against the asphalt. The moment he was on the side street, he saw something he didn't like.

A truck.

It wasn't right in the middle of the road, but the front end was jutting out from the parking space in front of a motorcycle repair shop.

Lucas hit his brakes.

"You think someone's inside the truck?" Hailey asked. Her voice was shaking like the rest of her.

Lucas didn't know, and it was next to impossible to see inside the truck's cab. There was a streetlight and a lit sign for the motorcycle shop, but the tint was so dark on the windshield that he couldn't tell. He pulled up a little farther though so he could get a better look at the front license plates.

"Out-of-state plates," he mumbled under his breath.

Maybe that in itself meant nothing, but Lucas got that feeling in his gut. The feeling that told him to get the heck out of there.

He threw the SUV into Reverse.

But the second he did that, the truck door opened, and a man bolted out.

The guy had a rifle.

"Get down," Lucas repeated to Hailey. "And this time, stay there."

Whether she would or not was anyone's

guess, but he didn't want to have to worry about her being shot. He hit the gas, the SUV speeding backward. But he didn't get out of the path of that rifleman fast enough.

The bullet slammed into the windshield.

Since this wasn't the vehicle he used for work, the glass wasn't reinforced. The shot tore through the safety glass, the bullet exiting out the back.

Great. Just great.

Now he had two thugs after them, and Lucas had no choice but to go back in the direction he'd seen that other shooter in the park. Maybe the guy was long gone by now. Or better yet, maybe one of the deputies had managed to capture him.

When Lucas reached the side street, he spun the SUV around so he could drive forward. He definitely didn't want to head right into the middle of an ambush, so he headed for a better lit area.

"The truck's coming after us," Hailey said.

And that's when he realized she'd lifted her head and was looking out the side window.

Lucas pushed her right back down. "Don't make it easier for them to kill you," he snapped. Yeah, it was harsh, but Hailey was clearly the target of some very determined attackers.

Whoever was in the truck fired another shot

at them, this one slamming into the rear end of the SUV. A second shot quickly followed.

Then a third.

"There must be two of them," Hailey muttered. She hadn't figured that out by looking at them, though. She was still on the floor.

But Lucas knew there had to be two, as well. Those shots were too well aimed for someone who was trying to negotiate the turns and dodging the cars parked along the street.

"Hang on," Lucas told her a split second before he turned onto another side street. He was thankful he'd grown up here and knew these streets like the back of his hand.

His phone buzzed, and since Hailey still had hold of it, she answered it and put it on speaker.

"Where are you?" he heard Grayson immediately ask. "Someone just called about shots being fired near Henderson's Motorcycle Shop."

"Someone in a blue pickup is shooting at us. We're on Bluebonnet Street, coming up near the Corral Bar." It was a risk since there'd be customers still inside, but Lucas didn't plan on stopping or even slowing down. "I'll turn back on Main Street and head in your direction. Please tell me you found the first shooter."

"Not yet. But I'll send Dade and Josh your way to help," Grayson said, and he ended the call.

Good. Dade and Josh were both cousins,

both deputy sheriffs, and maybe having backup would cause these thugs to quit firing.

The parking lot of the Corral Bar was lit up better than the rest of the street, and Lucas glanced in his side mirror at the truck. Definitely two men. And the one on the passenger side was doing the shooting.

"I can return fire," Hailey insisted, already climbing into the seat and lowering the window. "Please don't stop me. This is all my fault, and I have to do something to stop them."

"No way." And he meant it. It might indeed be partially her fault for not coming to him sooner, but she wasn't sticking her neck out to fire any shots.

Hailey didn't get a chance to argue with him. That's because the sound of sirens stopped anything she was about to say. In the distance, behind the truck, Lucas saw the flashing blue lights of a police cruiser.

Dade and Josh, no doubt.

The driver stopped following Lucas and took a very quick turn off a side street. A street that would lead them straight to the highway.

No, hell, no.

Lucas didn't want these clowns getting away, but it wasn't smart to go in pursuit with Hailey in the vehicle. Besides, Dade and Josh went after them, and Lucas could only hope they'd catch them.

"Keep watch for the other shooter," Lucas told Hailey.

He hated to rely on her for help, but with the glass in the front, back and side windows cracked and webbed, they had reduced visibility. That would make it hard for them to see the guy hiding between one of the buildings where he could shoot at them as they drove by.

Lucas held his breath, going as fast as he could, and he didn't release that breath until he made it back onto Main Street. Definitely no sign of the shooter, so he headed for the sheriff's office.

"Can you run?" he asked her.

"I'll try," she assured him. Which meant she couldn't. "I had to use a cane to walk to your SUV."

Definitely couldn't.

The SUV squealed to a stop directly in front of the door to the sheriff's office, but he didn't get out. Lucas waited until Grayson hurried to the door and threw it open.

"I'm carrying you in," Lucas insisted, and he didn't leave any room for argument.

He scooped her up in his arms and rushed her inside the building, with Grayson locking the door behind them. But Lucas didn't stop there.

He hurried her past the squad room to the hall that led to Grayson's office and the break room. That way, if someone did come in with guns blazing, she'd have some protection.

"Dade and Josh are in pursuit," Lucas told Grayson. "Arizona plates, but there was something covering the numbers. Mud, I think." Probably not an accident.

"Arizona?" Hailey repeated.

Lucas knew the reason for her concern. De-Salvo had been from Arizona, which meant his son, Eric, likely was, too. So, had Eric sent those goons after Hailey?

Now that they weren't in the SUV, Lucas got a better look at her. Especially a better look at the fear in her eyes. And the fact that she was having to grip the door to steady herself.

"As soon as it's safe, I'll have the doctor come over to see you," Lucas told her.

But she was shaking her head before he even finished. "I can't trust Dr. Parton. Or anyone in the hospital. Someone planted that bug on the table next to my bed."

Lucas certainly hadn't forgotten about that. The device needed to be checked, but that would have to wait, because Grayson no doubt had every available deputy on this manhunt for the shooters.

"When there's time, Hailey will need to give you a statement," Lucas told Grayson.

Grayson nodded. He still had his gun drawn, was still keeping watch on the area just outside the building. "Is she in WITSEC?"

"Yes," Hailey answered. "But I don't want the marshals to know I'm here."

Grayson mumbled something Lucas didn't catch, but he didn't need to hear the words to know that Grayson wasn't pleased about all this going on right under his nose.

"Hell, you worked for me," Grayson added.

She nodded. "I figured it was a way to keep an eye on what was happening in town, just in case something went wrong." Hailey paused. "And something did go wrong."

Yeah. And Lucas wondered if sleeping with him was in that something-gone-wrong category.

"I'll call Mason and give him an update," Grayson said after he shot Hailey a glare.

Hailey dropped back a step, holding onto Grayson's desk. Lucas was volleying his attention between her and the outside. However, she got his complete attention when she made a soft gasp.

Lucas hurried to her, following her gaze to the computer on the desk. It was obviously the security feed that the doctor had sent Grayson.

In the shot, the tall, lanky man was coming through the glass doors of the ER. Grayson had paused it and zoomed in on the man's face.

Darrin Sandmire, no doubt.

Lucas had no trouble seeing the renewed fear in Hailey's eyes. "That's definitely the man who came to my house three months ago. And the man who ran me off the road that night."

Lucas hadn't needed to hear anything else about the guy to know that he wanted him caught, questioned and punished.

Hailey touched the screen to get the security feed moving again. Darrin disappeared from view when he walked past the camera and to the hall. Since it would have taken him several minutes to get to her room, Lucas sped up the footage, watching for Darrin to reemerge.

He did.

But the man wasn't alone.

There was a woman with him, walking right by his side, and it was obvious they were talking. The woman was a blonde, and she kept her head down. Right until she was close to the camera.

Now Hailey's gasp wasn't so soft.

"I know her. That's Colleen Jeffrey."

The name meant nothing to Lucas, and he didn't recognize her, either. "Who is she?"

There were tears shimmering in Hailey's eyes when she looked up at him. "My half sister."

Damn.

Lucas was about to assure her that maybe this was a coincidence. But it didn't look like that to him. He needed to get this woman in for questioning right away.

He heard the footsteps. Hurried ones, and they put Lucas right back on alert again. Though he hadn't exactly been relaxing.

"We've got a problem," Grayson said, stepping into the doorway. "Someone tripped the security sensor near the back fence at the ranch. One of the ranch hands spotted a gunman."

Chapter Four

Hailey's breath froze. She wanted to scream, to shout out for Lucas to hurry to the ranch so they could protect their son, but the words and sounds were wedged there in her throat.

No. This couldn't be happening. This monster couldn't get to her baby.

Even without her warning, Lucas thankfully understood just how dangerous a situation this could be, because he took off running toward the front of the building. Hailey followed him. Or rather, she tried.

Lucas must have remembered she was still hobbling, because he spun around, scooped her up in his arms and hurried toward his shot-up SUV still parked just outside the door.

"We need to use a cruiser," Grayson called out to them. "Because this could be a trap to lure you into the open."

Lucas stopped, and while everything inside

Hailey wanted to move, to hurry to the ranch, she knew Grayson was right.

"Wait right here for me," Grayson insisted. "I'll bring the cruiser around to the front."

Hailey didn't want to waste precious minutes while he did that, but they didn't have many options here. Lucas and she waited, the time crawling by slower than a snail's pace, and it seemed to take an eternity for Grayson to drive up. Even before the cruiser came to a stop, Lucas and she jumped into the backseat, and Grayson took off again.

"I'll call the ranch and get an update," Lucas said.

As much as she wanted to know what was going on, Hailey didn't want anyone there distracted right now. She wanted all the focus on protecting the baby.

Camden.

The name seemed foreign to her. Probably because she'd yet to see her son, but maybe that would change soon. Maybe they'd get to the ranch and put an end to the danger.

"Tillie," Lucas said to whoever answered his call.

"One of the nannies," Grayson provided to Hailey, but he didn't even glance back at her when he spoke. He looked all around, no doubt in case someone was trying to follow them.

Or attack them again.

Hailey couldn't hear what the nanny was saying, but since Lucas's arm was pressed against her, she felt his muscles relax just a little. "We'll be there as fast as we can." He paused. "Hailey's with me."

The nanny perhaps hadn't even heard she was out of the coma, so this could be a real shock. An unwanted one. Hailey didn't know Tillie, but she doubted she was going to get a warm reception from anyone at the Silver Creek Ranch. It wouldn't matter that she thought she'd done the right thing.

Still did think that.

But a family of lawmen wouldn't see it that way. They would believe she should have trusted them. However, maybe they could see now that all the trust in the world wouldn't have put an end to the danger.

Oh, mercy.

That reminder came at her hard, like a heavyweight's fist. The reason she'd tried to escape was to avoid this. To keep her child safe. And now he wasn't safe because of her.

"Whoever's behind the attacks will use Camden to get to me," Hailey said under her breath.

She hadn't intended to say that aloud, and it stung even more when Lucas made a sound of agreement. He'd finished his call with the nanny and now was keeping watch. Along with glancing at her.

"That doesn't mean you're going to try to take him and disappear," Lucas snapped. There wasn't a shred of gentleness in his tone. In fact, it was the same tone he likely used with criminal suspects.

"It's too late to take him and hide," Hailey agreed. "Too late for me to disappear, as well. Because now that they know I'm awake, they won't stop, and they'll try to use the baby to come after me."

That meant she needed to find out who *they* were. And fast. For that to happen, she needed to rely on Lucas.

Something that wouldn't please him.

It didn't please her, either, but no one would work harder than Lucas to keep Camden safe. Of course, once that happened, and this snake was captured and behind bars, Lucas and she would have another battle to fight.

For custody.

But that was a fight that would have to wait for another day. Right now, Hailey had enough to deal with.

"The fences are all rigged with security alarms?" she asked.

"Yeah," Grayson and Lucas answered at the same time. It was Lucas who continued. "There are also sensors on the grounds. Cameras, too. Since this clown tripped a sensor, the ranch hands and my cousins will be able to pinpoint his exact location before he can get near one of the houses."

Good. But pinpointing him wasn't the same as stopping the threat.

"Hurry," Hailey said to Grayson. She was speaking purely out of frustration, because he was going as fast as he safely could.

The rural roads that led to the ranch weren't exactly straight. Plenty of sharp curves and turns, and it certainly wouldn't help them if Grayson wrecked.

Something she knew all too well.

Hailey couldn't quite choke back a gasp when the cruiser tires squealed around one of those turns and it felt as if Grayson was losing control of the vehicle. All the memories of that other night came flooding back.

The frantic rush to get away from the person trying to kill her. The adrenaline and the fear. Even the feeling of the impact.

The pain.

But more intense than the pain and the fear had been the sickening dread that she'd failed.

"Flashbacks?" Lucas asked.

She nodded. "I remember that you're the one who found me that night. If it hadn't been you…"

Hailey didn't finish that thought. No need. Lucas had found her, and while it hadn't made things perfect, it had allowed her to deliver the baby safely.

Grayson took the final turn, and Hailey saw the ranch come into view. To say it was sprawling was an understatement. It'd been huge, but now that the Ryland cousins were buying up the adjacent land and building their own homes, the place stretched out for miles and miles.

They'd also added more security since the last time she'd visited. There was now a large security gate, and she saw several men near it. Ranch hands, probably, since she didn't recognize any of them.

"Get down," Lucas told her as they approached the gate. He lowered the window. "Anything?" he asked the men.

"Yep. Just a few seconds ago Sawyer called to say he shot at a guy who'd crossed over the fence. He and two of the other hands are chasing him."

Hailey sucked in her breath. Sawyer was his cousin as well as an FBI agent. "Did Sawyer have to fire shots anywhere near the houses?"

The guy volleyed glances among Lucas,

Grayson and her. Maybe he was trying to figure out if it was okay if he answered since he probably didn't even know who she was.

"No, the shooting happened in the back pasture," the guy said after Lucas gave him a go-ahead nod. "Mason said, though, that y'all should wait down here until they've made sure there's only one."

Oh, mercy.

As hard as that was to hear—and it was even harder for her to stay put—Hailey knew he was right. The attacker might not be alone. Heck, he could have brought an entire army with him, and it was best to aim that army at her rather than launch an attack near the houses.

Still, waiting was hard.

Even if she lifted her head, something Lucas wouldn't like her to do, Hailey couldn't see Lucas's house from this part of the road, but she knew it was less than a half mile away. She knew because he'd taken her there for the one night they'd been together. The night she'd had a serious lapse in judgment and gotten way too personal with a man she should have avoided. Or so it'd seemed at the time. But without that night, she wouldn't have her son, and despite everything that'd gone on, the one thing she was certain of was that she loved her baby.

Lucas didn't seem to be having an easier time

waiting than she was. He put the window back up, mumbled some profanity and took out his phone. This time she saw that he was calling the nanny again.

"Just checking to make sure everything is okay," Lucas said when Tillie answered.

Hailey automatically scooted closer so she could hear what the nanny had to say, but that only earned her a scowl from Lucas. He put the call on speaker, her cue to inch away from him. She did.

"The baby's fine," Tillie assured Lucas. "He went straight to sleep after his bottle. And Mason's still here just in case."

Just in case everything went from bad to worse. Hailey hated that it was a possibility, but Mason was another lawman, so it was good to have him there. She prayed, though, that he wouldn't be needed and that the danger would end soon. With this idiot intruder not just in custody but also willing to tell them the name of the person who'd hired him.

"You said earlier that Hailey was with you," Tillie went on. She paused. "Is, uh, everything okay? Did that man try to get onto the ranch because of her?"

"Yeah," Lucas admitted. Now he was the one who paused. "I'll need to take the baby someplace safe. Will you be able to come with us?"

"Of course," Tillie quickly agreed.

Hailey was shaking her head before the nanny even answered.

The head shaking caused Lucas to scowl again. "I'm going to protect my son," he snarled as if she didn't want the same thing.

She did. More than anything, she wanted him safe. Lucas and his family, too. "But I want to see him."

That got Lucas's muscles tightening again. "And then what?"

It was a good question. Hailey didn't have anything resembling a good answer. "I don't know," she admitted. "I need some answers, and I think the place to start is with my sister."

"I agree," Lucas said without hesitation. "I'll want her contact info and anything recent you have on her. I'll especially want to know why she could want you dead."

"I don't know any of those things," Hailey had to admit. "I haven't seen or heard from Colleen since I've been in WITSEC."

Lucas huffed, clearly not pleased that she hadn't given him something to go on. "You two were close?"

"Once." But that was another round of bad memories. "We were both working as computer systems analysts for Preston DeSalvo's company. I testified against him, but Colleen didn't.

She claimed she didn't see the incriminating evidence that I found."

Lucas jumped right on that. "She lied?"

"Maybe. But I can't believe she'd be the one behind this. I'm still her sister."

He gave her a flat look. "Cain and Abel were brothers, and you know how that ended."

Yes, with one murdering the other, but Hailey had to hang on to something, and that something was that her only sister hadn't betrayed her like this. Still, she wanted to talk to Colleen and get this all sorted out.

She nearly reached for his phone to make a call, but there was no one who came to mind that she could trust. Well, no one other than Lucas.

"I'll bring Colleen in for questioning," Lucas said as if reading her mind. He didn't get a chance to add anything else because the sound got their attention.

A shot.

Even though it was in the distance, it still caused Hailey's heart to slam against her chest. She held her breath, waiting, and even though she tried to steel herself for whatever would happen next, she still gasped when Lucas's phone buzzed.

"Mason," he said looking at the screen before he answered it and put the call on speaker.

She hadn't thought her heart could beat any faster, but she'd obviously been wrong. Mason was with the baby, and if he was calling then maybe that meant the shot had been fired close to the house.

Or in it.

Hailey pressed her fingers to her mouth and listened, praying.

"Sawyer fired the shot," Mason said. "The guy's alive for now."

"Is he talking?" Lucas asked.

"No, but I just called an ambulance, so maybe he'll say something on the way to the hospital. Sawyer has a way of getting dirt to talk."

Good. But that didn't mean this was over. "Are there any other attackers out there?" Hailey pressed.

Just as the ranch hand had done, Mason hesitated. "No. Nothing else is showing up on any of the security feeds, either. It looks as if this clown came alone. And I don't think he came here to kill anybody. He had surveillance equipment on him."

So there could be others on the way. It was too much to hope that this guy's injury and arrest would get the person behind this to back off.

"It's safe for you to come to the house," Mason continued. "If you want to come, that is."

She knew what he meant by that. Mason was giving his cousin an out in case Lucas didn't want her to see the baby. Hailey was about to insist that happen when Lucas gave Grayson the go-ahead to get moving.

Toward the house.

Hailey sat back up, keeping watch around them, but she was also looking for the house. It finally came into view since it was the first building on the ranch road. All of the interior lights were off, probably as a safety precaution, but there were security lights on all four corners of the property. Enough for her to see the barn and corral that hadn't been there a year ago.

Lucas was making this place a home.

Part of her was thankful for that. Their son deserved it. But she was betting there was no place in this home for her.

Grayson pulled to a stop directly in front of the porch, and the door opened. Mason. Yet another unfriendly face, but then, Mason usually looked unfriendly. As he'd done at the sheriff's office, Lucas got her in—fast. This time, though, he didn't carry her. He looped his arm around her waist to steady her, and the moment they were inside, he moved away from her.

Hailey immediately looked around for the baby. But there was no sign of him or the nanny.

She was about to demand to see him, but Mason stepped in front of her.

"Just got a text from Sawyer," Mason said, his voice low and dangerous. "The guy he shot is drifting in and out of consciousness, but this is what the guy said."

He held his phone screen up for her to see, and the words there caused her to drop back a step.

Hailey Darrow paid me to take the kid.

Chapter Five

Lucas didn't know who looked more shocked by the accusation that the wounded gunman had just made. He or Hailey.

"I didn't," she said, her gaze firing between Mason and him. "I only left the hospital a couple of hours ago."

Mason didn't seem convinced. "You were conscious for a week. You could have called someone and set this whole thing up."

The anger flared through Hailey's eyes, and she opened her mouth as if ready to return verbal fire, but she was obviously spent. Heck, so was Lucas, and while part of him hated to defend the woman who'd tried to run from him, he couldn't see how this would have played out.

"There was no phone in her hospital room," Lucas explained. "And yes, she could have borrowed one from someone on the staff, but that kind of thing doesn't stay a secret very long."

Lucas could have gone on and mentioned the part about Hailey not having touched her bank accounts since she'd been in the coma, and it wasn't as if she'd had wads of cash lying around the hospital to pay someone to carry through on something like this.

Even Lucas's own explanation didn't seem to convince Mason. "You trust her, then?" Mason asked.

"No," Lucas readily admitted. "But if Hailey intended to take the baby, she wouldn't have done it this way."

At least, he hoped like the devil that she wouldn't. The baby and other members of his family could have been hurt by the thug who'd trespassed onto the ranch.

"Thank you," Hailey said to him.

For some reason, that riled Lucas. Maybe because he didn't want to do anything for her that would cause her to say something like that.

"So, who did hire the *lying* sack of dirt?" Mason asked.

Hailey shook her head, but it was clear from the way she was looking around that her attention was elsewhere. She obviously wanted to see the baby, and Lucas tried to remind himself that if their positions were reversed, he would have wanted the same thing.

Of course, their positions would never be reversed because he would have never gone on the run from the law.

"I'll question Hailey's sister, Colleen, and Eric DeSalvo in the morning." Lucas tipped his head to the hall that led to the bedrooms. "Is Tillie in the nursery?"

Mason lowered his phone and nodded. Even though he didn't voice his disapproval as to what was about to happen, it was on his face. "I'll wait here until I get the all-clear from Sawyer."

Lucas thanked him and made a mental note to thank all the others who'd pulled together to keep Camden safe. For now, though, he had to focus on getting through this. And *this* was having Hailey see the baby.

From the moment Camden had been born, Lucas had known it might come down to this. But as every day had passed with Hailey in a coma, he'd also considered that she might never wake up. That she might never have a claim on their child. Now, here she was, and Lucas was having to face one of his worst fears.

That he might lose his son.

Not to a kidnapper, either. But to Hailey. She wouldn't be able to get full custody of Camden. No way would Lucas allow that, but she would be entitled to visitation rights. Considering she was in WITSEC, that was going to be tricky. And not very safe for any of them.

Moving ahead of her, Lucas led her down the hall. She caught onto the side of the wall to steady herself, and she was probably moving as fast as she could go.

When they reached the nursery, Lucas stepped in, his gaze immediately connecting with the nanny's. There was just as much concern in Tillie's expression as there had been in Mason's. But she stepped aside so that Lucas—and Hailey—had the crib in their direct line of sight.

Where Camden was sleeping.

"I'll be in the living room if you need me," Tillie said, but her offer seemed to be a question, as if maybe he wanted her to stay.

Lucas nodded, giving her the go-ahead to leave, but Hailey didn't wait for Tillie to be out the door before she hobbled her way to the crib. The sound that left her mouth crushed at his heart. Part moan, part sigh.

All love.

It was a sound and a look that Lucas felt all too well because he got that same punch of emotion every time he was near his son. And even when he wasn't.

"He's so beautiful," Hailey whispered, touching her fingers to the wispy strands of dark brown hair.

Lucas had to agree with her, but he was certain that was the reaction of most parents. Certain, too, that Hailey would want to do more than just touch his hair. She looked back at him, as if waiting for permission. She didn't wait long, though, before she scooped Camden up in her arms.

She made that sound again and kissed his cheek. Even though Camden stirred a little, he went right back to sleep. Good. Even though his son was too young to know what was going on, Lucas didn't want to risk Camden being upset by having his sleep interrupted. He also didn't want to risk Hailey falling with the child, and since her legs were obviously still wobbly, he helped her to the nearby chair.

"Is he healthy?" she asked.

"Yeah." It was hard for him to talk about something so—well—normal. "He's right on target for his height, weight and milestones."

She nodded and looked up at him, and that's when he saw the tears in her eyes. "I was so scared that he'd been hurt in the accident."

"He could have been," Lucas quickly pointed out, but then instantly regretted the jab. It was the truth, but stating the obvious didn't make him feel any better.

"I know. I'm so sorry. When I ran, my only thought was to keep him safe."

Lucas nearly went for another jab by reminding her that the safe thing to do would have been to come to him, but that ship had already sailed. They were here now and had to deal with this. Not just the danger, either. But all those old feelings.

He'd been attracted to her once and vice versa. That's what had landed them in bed in the first place. And while there were still some lingering traces of the attraction, it wouldn't play into this. He hoped the bitterness he felt over what'd happened wouldn't, either. Right now, bitterness wouldn't help.

He was about to question her more about the night of the accident, to see if she remembered any details that would help them find out who was responsible for the attacks, but Hailey spoke before he did.

"Tell me about the delivery," she said.

Lucas paused, not because he intended to hold anything back, but because remembering that night still felt like a punch to the gut.

"I was scared," he admitted. "We didn't know if there'd been trauma to the baby, and since you were so close to your due date, the docs did a C-section on you. But everything turned out okay. Everything except that you were in a coma," Lucas added.

She, too, paused. Then nodded. "I've heard that some people remember and hear things while they're in comas. I didn't." She brushed another kiss on Camden's cheek. "I wish I could remember seeing him as a newborn. He's already so big."

Camden was, but while Hailey had indeed missed a lot, the baby wasn't old enough to have noticed that his mom hadn't been around.

Hailey looked up at Lucas again, those tears still shimmering in her eyes. "I know this is hard for you. You haven't had to share him with anyone for the past three months."

Lucas wasn't sure how to respond to that and didn't get a chance to say anything anyway, because Mason appeared in the doorway. One look at his cousin's face and Lucas knew something else had gone wrong. Apparently so did Hailey, because she slowly got to her feet, her attention nailed to Mason.

"The gunman died on the way to the hospital," Mason said.

Hell. Lucas had wanted him alive so they could get answers. But maybe they could still do that. "Did he have a phone on him? Maybe his boss's number is in his contacts?"

Mason nodded. "Grayson will check for that,

but there's more." He paused. "The ranch hands did a thorough search of the fence line in that back part of the ranch, and it appears the dead thug didn't come alone. There were enough tracks back there for three people."

Lucas bit back the profanity that he nearly blurted out, something he'd been training himself to do now that he was a father. Still, it was hard not to curse about that. "Any other signs of the men?"

"No. They're apparently gone. For now, anyway."

That didn't mean they wouldn't be back. Maybe even tonight, since the darkness would give them an advantage for an attack.

"I've got men patrolling the entire ranch," Mason went on. "I also called everyone and told them to lock down and stay inside."

By "everyone" he meant his brothers and their cousins. No one would be leaving and coming onto the ranch unless Mason gave the okay. Which he wouldn't do until he was certain it was safe. And Lucas knew what that meant.

This time he wasn't able to stop himself from cursing.

Because it meant Hailey would have to stay there.

Of course, he probably wouldn't have been

able to talk her into budging since she'd want to be near the baby, but Lucas had planned on having her sleep far away from the Silver Creek Ranch. Far away from Camden, too.

"I'm so sorry," Hailey whispered. Maybe she was apologizing again for the danger. But one look in her eyes and Lucas knew the reason for this "I'm sorry." She had also figured out what the sleeping arrangements would be.

"You can stay in the guest room," Lucas growled. It was at the end of the hall, as far away as he could get her while still having her under the same roof.

Hailey mumbled a thanks, and while Lucas thought part of her looked relieved, that was still fear he saw in her eyes. Worry, too. Especially worry when she looked at Mason again. His cousin wasn't budging. Mason continued to stand there, his hands bracketed on the doorjamb.

"What else happened?" Hailey asked Mason. Her voice was shaky again, probably because she knew they were about to get another dose of bad news.

"Grayson tried to get in touch with Colleen, so he could bring her in for questioning." Mason paused again. "But there's a problem. Colleen is missing."

HAILEY HOPED THIS medical exam wasn't a mistake.

She wasn't certain about the ER physician, Dr. Parton, but Lucas had assured her that Parton wasn't the one who'd planted that bug in her hospital room, that the doctor was trustworthy. So, that's what Hailey was going to do—trust him. Besides, she needed to make sure she was okay. Not just for her sake but to soothe some of the concern on Lucas's face.

Of course, she had plenty of her own concerns, too.

There were so many things for her to worry about, and that's what she'd done through the night and now the morning. The constant threat of an attack. Her missing sister. The obvious tension between Lucas and her. Between her and his family, too.

But it was hard for Hailey to focus solely on all of that when she was looking at her son's face while Lucas was holding him.

For the entire time she'd carried him, she had considered how he might look. Considered as well the love she would feel for him, but she'd way underestimated that love. She couldn't believe how deep it was for this child, and even though it crushed her heart, she knew that same feeling of love was the very reason that Lucas would do everything to hang on to his child.

Everything, including attempts to exclude her.

Those attempts wouldn't work, of course. Or maybe they wouldn't. If they couldn't stop the threat of another attack, then she might have no choice but to disappear. She'd do that if it meant keeping Camden safe.

She'd started that process by using Lucas's laptop and putting in her password for the storage cloud for the files she'd gathered on Eric DeSalvo. It'd be a few more hours before she could open them, but once Lucas had a chance to go over them, maybe he could find something he could use to arrest Eric. It might not put an end to the attacks, but at least it would get him off the streets for a while.

"Follow the light with your eyes," Dr. Parton instructed her.

Hailey did, though it meant taking her attention off her son. And Lucas. Lucas was feeding the baby his bottle while he had his phone sandwiched between his shoulder and his ear. She wasn't sure who was on the other end of the phone line this time, but Lucas had obviously adapted to juggling his work with fatherhood.

"From what I can tell, you're fine," the doctor said, stepping back from her. "You'll need a thorough exam, though, and some tests that I can do only at the hospital. Any idea when it'll be okay for that?"

It was the million-dollar question, and Hailey didn't have a clue what the answer was. She shook her head. "We're waiting on some information." Information that would ideally lead to an arrest.

The doctor didn't seem especially pleased with an indefinite delay to those tests, and Hailey knew why. There could be brain damage. And damage to her legs. The muscles felt a little stronger, but she was nowhere near a hundred percent and might need physical therapy to regain all her strength. No way could she risk going to PT or taking those tests now, though, and she didn't want to speculate how long it would be before that happened.

The doctor gathered his things and headed to the door, where Mason was waiting to escort him back to town. They left, leaving Hailey to sit there and watch as Camden finished his bottle. As if it were the most natural thing in the world, Lucas put the bottle aside and moved the baby to his shoulder to burp him.

A year ago, if someone had told her that the tough cowboy cop would be the doting father, she wouldn't have believed it. Lucas likely wouldn't have, either.

Tillie came out of the kitchen and made eye contact with Lucas. "You want me to take him?" Tillie mouthed.

"No, thanks. I'm finished with my call." He put away his phone and looked at Hailey. "That was Grayson. Still no word on your sister, but Eric DeSalvo should be arriving at the sheriff's office any minute now."

Good. Hailey figured the best place to start with getting those answers would be with Eric. And Colleen. It sickened her to think that her sister might be involved in this.

"What about the other gunmen who were around the ranch last night?" she asked. "Any signs of them?"

"No. And the dead guy, Darrin, was using a burner cell phone and didn't have any contacts stored there. In fact, the phone hadn't been used, so there's nothing to trace."

Another dead end. Literally. Since Darrin had lived only long enough to accuse her of hiring him.

"Grayson had the medics take Darrin's picture," Lucas went on. When he reached to take his phone from his jeans pocket, it caused the baby to move, and Camden stirred, lifting his head just a little.

Hailey figured Camden was too young to see her from across the room, so she went closer. Lucas didn't scowl, exactly, but it was close. He took out his phone and handed it to her.

"Take a look at the picture Grayson sent, and

see if you recognize Darrin. Is he the same man who went after you the night you were trying to get away?"

She took the phone, her fingers brushing against his. Lucas noticed. Noticed, too, that she was volleying glances between the baby and him. He pulled in a long, weary breath.

"Sit down," he growled. "You can hold Camden while you tell me about the picture."

Hailey moved as fast as she could, making her way back to the chair. Lucas went to her, easing the baby into her arms.

There it was again. That punch of emotion.

Though it was hard to focus with Camden staring up at her, Hailey studied the photo. It wasn't the best shot since the man's face was twisted with pain, but Hailey picked through the features.

And remembered.

She sucked in her breath so fast that she nearly got choked. "He definitely looks like the man who ran me off the road."

Other memories came flooding back. The car following her. Her frantic attempt to get away. Then the crash.

"He rammed into the back of my car, forcing me into a ditch," she explained. "That's when I hit my head."

Thank goodness she'd been wearing a seat

belt. That had prevented her from being thrown from the car, but it hadn't stopped the tree limb from coming through the windshield and hitting her.

Lucas stared at her, clearly waiting for more details. Hailey had more, but she had to fight the panicky feeling rising in her again. It wasn't that night, but it suddenly felt as if it was.

"After I crashed, Darrin came to the side of the car," Hailey continued. "He looked at me." But then she stopped, her attention going back to Lucas. "Why didn't he just kill me then? I was helpless, barely conscious."

"Maybe he didn't want you dead," Lucas said. "He probably wanted those computer files and would have been willing to torture you to get them."

Yes. That had to be it. "But he didn't get a chance to kidnap me, because that's about the time you drove up. Did you see Darrin leave?"

"I saw his SUV speeding away. I couldn't go in pursuit."

That's because she had needed medical attention ASAP. Lucas had saved her life. Camden's, too, by staying with them. Lucas didn't seem any more comfortable thinking about that night than she did, and he looked relieved when Tillie came back into the living room.

"Is Camden ready for his bath?" the nanny

asked, her voice tentative, probably because she knew that Hailey wanted to continue holding him.

Lucas nodded. "Best if he sticks to his routine," he told Hailey. "Plus, we need to do reports for the attack."

Yes, paperwork. Necessary, but she still hated having to hand her son over to the nanny. She'd gotten so few minutes holding him. Of course, a lifetime would be too few.

"You can watch," Tillie added, glancing at Hailey. "That way, you'll know how to do it." She also glanced at Lucas, and Tillie seemed to ignore the slight scowl that was on his face.

Maybe a scowl because it would mean a delay in doing those reports, but also because Tillie was including her.

Hailey didn't give Lucas a chance to veto Tillie's offer. She stood, following the woman as best she could to the bathroom just across the hall from the nursery. Lucas followed, too. Good thing, because just before Hailey reached the door, she stumbled and would have fallen flat on her face if Lucas hadn't caught her.

And just like that, she was in his arms.

The memories came. No way to stop them. Not with Lucas and her being body to body. Hailey got some flashes of even more body contact. Of when they were naked in bed.

Mercy, that caused the heat to flood through her again. Worse, Lucas noticed, and he looked as if he wanted to curse again. He didn't. He moved her away from him. Well, he moved so that her breasts were no longer pressed against his chest, but he looped his arm around her waist to steady her.

"You should be resting," he grumbled.

"Would you rest if you were in my shoes?" she countered.

That only deepened his scowl. Both knew the answer to that—no, he wouldn't.

Lucas kept his arm around her when they went to the doorway, but it was obvious that he was trying to touch as little of her as possible. Hailey soon didn't notice it because her attention was on the baby. Or at least, it was until Lucas's phone buzzed. She was close enough to see Grayson's name on the screen.

She felt the muscles in Lucas's arm tense. Probably because this could be bad news. He stepped back into the hall, answered the call and put it on speaker.

"Is Hailey there?" Grayson said without even issuing a greeting. Yes, this was bad news. Hailey could tell from his tone.

"I'm here," she answered.

"San Antonio PD found your sister," Grayson continued.

"Where is she?" Hailey immediately asked.

"The hospital. She's hurt, and she's asking to see you. Colleen says she knows who's trying to kill you."

Chapter Six

A car accident.

That's what had put Colleen in the hospital. And not just any ordinary accident, but one that'd happened on the same stretch of road where Hailey had nearly been killed. Lucas figured that was either an eerie coincidence or someone was trying to send them a message.

If it was a message, Lucas hadn't needed it. He knew just how much danger they were in. That's why it was almost certainly a mistake to take Hailey off the ranch and to the hospital, with the threat of an attack still hanging over their heads. But he also knew this meeting with Colleen could give them critical information to put an end to the danger.

Maybe an immediate end.

If Colleen confessed to helping Darrin when he tried to run Hailey off the road.

Lucas doubted that would actually happen,

but he wouldn't rule it out. Heck, he wasn't ruling out anything right now. After all, he'd sworn that Hailey would never be under his roof again, and she'd not only spent the night there but also was back in his arms. Sort of. As he'd done earlier, he had to help her out of the cruiser, and that involved touching her.

He didn't have to remind her to hurry, and she did. As much as a hobbling woman could hurry. Lucas only hoped all this moving around wasn't doing anything to harm her leg muscles. The sooner he put some physical distance between them, the better, and that started with her getting back to a hundred percent.

Lucas believed her story about someone trying to kill her. And he felt a little sorry for her. But he wasn't ready to welcome her back into his and Camden's lives.

There was a deputy at the door to the hospital. Another inside. Since his cousins Dade and Gage had escorted Lucas and Hailey to the hospital, that meant Grayson had three other lawmen plus himself tied up with this.

"Thank you for not saying it was a stupid idea for me to come here," Hailey whispered as they made their way down the hall.

Lucas glanced at her from the corner of his eye. "Just because I didn't say it doesn't mean I agree with this. You could have demanded that Colleen tell you everything over the phone."

She glanced at him, too. "I did demand," she reminded him.

Yeah, but Hailey hadn't stood her ground when Colleen had insisted that she speak to her sister in person. This felt like a trap, and while the baby wasn't in danger at the moment, Hailey clearly was.

When they reached the patient ward of the hospital, Lucas spotted yet another lawman cousin. Josh. But he wasn't alone. There was a lanky, dark-haired guy in a black suit standing next to him. Judging from their scowls, neither Josh nor the suit were happy.

Hailey had an equally unhappy reaction to the man. She sucked in her breath. "That's Brian Minton. He was one of the FBI agents who worked on the DeSalvo investigation."

Even though they were only a few yards from Minton, Lucas stopped. "You don't trust him?"

The question was valid, considering Lucas could feel Hailey's suddenly tight muscles. She hadn't exactly been relaxed on the trip over, but the tension was even worse now.

"I don't trust anyone involved in that," Hailey answered without taking her attention off Minton. "Remember, Preston DeSalvo had a dirty agent on his payroll. I'm positive of that."

No way could Lucas forget it, especially now that he'd read the file about it. The problem was, there'd been at least a dozen agents involved in that case and countless others who might have distanced themselves from it just so there'd be no obvious connection to the DeSalvo family.

"Any proof that Minton's dirty?" Lucas pressed.

"No," Hailey readily admitted, and she got moving again. "What are you doing here?" she asked the agent.

"I've asked him the same thing," Josh provided. "I've also told him he's not getting into Colleen's room until I get the okay from the sheriff. I haven't gotten that okay," he added, directing his glare at Minton.

Minton tapped his badge. "I'm here to interview two witnesses—Colleen and Laura—or, rather, Hailey, as she's going by these days. This investigation belongs to the FBI."

"How do you figure that?" Lucas said, but he didn't wait for an explanation. "Hailey is in WITSEC, and the marshals are in charge of that. As for Colleen, she was in a car accident in the jurisdiction of the Silver Creek Sheriff's Office."

Minton gave him a blank stare and huffed. "You and I both know this is connected to the DeSalvo family."

Lucas almost hoped this guy was dirty just so he could arrest him. "I know no such thing. I'm just bringing Hailey here to visit her sister."

"A sister who could have information I need," Minton countered.

Welcome to the club, but Lucas was first in line to question Colleen.

"Who ran Colleen off the road?" Minton asked, volleying his gaze between Hailey and Lucas.

Lucas shrugged. "Don't have a clue. Yet. How about you? Do you know who did this?"

"Probably the same thug who caused Hailey's accident."

"That thug is dead," Lucas said. "He died last night. From what I understand, Colleen's accident happened hours later."

Judging from the startled look in Minton's eyes, he hadn't known that. Or else he was pretending not to have known. "Eric could be behind this," Minton added after a long pause.

Yes, he could be. Or Colleen. Or even Minton himself. Lucas kept his speculations to himself to see if Minton would continue. He did.

"Whoever did this had a chance to kill you that night," Minton reminded Hailey. "He might have had the same chance to kill Colleen. But he didn't take it." He paused. "Why?"

Hailey shook her head. "I don't know."

No more startled look in Minton's eyes, but the comment seemed to rile him. "There are rumors that you have some files. Files that could incriminate Eric. If you have something like that, it's illegal to withhold them."

Hailey didn't back down from the agent's suddenly lethal stare. "It's illegal only if I know about the files. I don't. Truth is, I have huge gaps in my memory."

Normally, Lucas hated lying and liars, but in this case, the lie was warranted. His gut told him to hold off on giving Minton anything until they'd sorted all of this out. The *sorting* began with Colleen.

"Once you get approval from the sheriff, I'll let you in to see her," Lucas said to Minton.

Minton protested, of course, but Josh blocked his way while Lucas ushered Hailey inside. Josh wouldn't let the agent in without a fight, but just in case that happened, Lucas stayed near the door. That meant letting go of Hailey while she stepped around him and turned toward her sister.

"Thank God you came," Colleen said.

Lucas had never met the woman, but he recognized her from the hospital surveillance tapes. Colleen was a blonde, and despite the fact that there were cuts and bruises on her face, she looked as if she'd recently combed her hair and put on some lipstick. That sent an uneasy feeling up his spine. People who'd just had a brush with death didn't usually think about their appearance.

Of course, maybe Colleen had faked the accident to make herself appear innocent.

"Laura, it's been so long," Colleen added.

"Hailey," she automatically corrected her. "I don't use Laura anymore." Hailey limped closer until she was finally able to catch onto the end of the bed for support. "Has anyone been in here who could have planted a bug in the room?"

Colleen's eyes widened, and then she shook her head. "Only the doctor and some nurses have come in to check on me. I would have noticed if they'd planted something."

Maybe, but just in case, Lucas took a look around. When he didn't find anything, he went back to his guarding duties.

"Did Minton leave?" Colleen asked, and it took Lucas a moment to realize she was talking to him. Since she hadn't asked for introductions, she likely knew who he was.

"He's still in the hall. The sheriff will stall him, but eventually he'll get in here to see you. Is that a problem?"

"Of course." Colleen didn't hesitate, either. "I don't trust any of the agents who helped put Preston behind bars."

Preston.

Interesting. Colleen certainly didn't say the man's name with the venom that Hailey did.

"Preston's dead," Colleen went on. "And Minton is one of the people responsible for that."

"Preston was killed in a prison fight," Lucas pointed out. "Are you saying that Minton arranged to have him killed?"

Colleen opened her mouth but then closed it just as quickly. "I don't know. But there was a lawman involved in the dirty stuff Preston was doing, and if I trust the wrong person, I could end up like Preston."

Yes, she could. So could Hailey, and it might happen even if she withheld that trust.

Hailey went a few more steps toward the bed and looked surprisingly steady. Maybe because she was trying to look strong for what was no doubt about to be a confrontation with her sister.

"Aren't you even going to ask me if I'm all right?" Colleen asked before Hailey could speak.

Hailey paused a long time. "Are you okay?"

"No," her sister snapped. "Someone tried to kill me." And she stared at Hailey as if she were somehow responsible for that.

"Are you going to ask me if I'm all right?" Hailey fired right back. Heck, she sounded stronger, too. "After all, I was in a coma, and not long after coming out of it, someone tried to kill me, too."

And she waited for Colleen to respond to that.

Lucas watched Colleen's expression and her body language, but the woman seemed clueless as to what was going on. Again though, she could have been playing dumb like the agent outside the door.

"The hospital surveillance footage," Lucas finally prompted her. "We saw you on it with the man who tried to kill Hailey."

Colleen gasped and pressed her fingers to her lips. "That man tried to kill my sister?"

"Not once but twice," Hailey confirmed.

Colleen gasped again and frantically shook her head. "He said he was a marshal, and he showed me a badge. It looked real."

"It was fake," Lucas told her. "And he was a hired gun. Any idea who he was working for?"

More head shaking from Colleen. "I honestly thought he was a marshal and that he was here to protect Hailey."

Hailey drew in a long, weary breath and sank down onto the foot of the bed. "Start from the beginning. We need to know everything about him, everything that he said to you."

There were tears shimmering in Colleen's eyes now, and while Lucas wasn't immune to those tears, he wasn't fully buying them just yet.

The woman could be crying because she'd just gotten caught and could be arrested.

"The marshal called me yesterday," Colleen started. "He said his name was Donald Silverman."

"It was Darrin Sandmire," Lucas corrected her.

"Was?" Colleen questioned.

"He's dead. Killed in a shoot-out with one of my cousins while he was attempting to get to Hailey."

Colleen pressed her fingertips to her mouth for a moment. "I didn't know. I swear I didn't," she added, her attention shifting to Hailey.

Like Lucas, Hailey still didn't look convinced. "This man asked you to meet him at the hospital?"

She nodded. "He said you were in danger, and that he needed my permission to access your personal things, like your computer."

So that he could get those files that Hailey had hidden. Files that Lucas needed to know more about as soon as they were finished here with Colleen.

"I told him that I didn't know where the rest of your personal things were," Colleen went on. "That the only things I had were what was collected from the car the night of your accident."

"It wasn't an accident," Hailey said. "That

man ran me off the road and put both my baby and me in grave danger."

Colleen blinked back the tears, and her expression changed a little. Not so much alarm on her face but concern. "You're not suggesting that I was working with this snake?"

Hailey stayed quiet a moment. "I only need to find out the truth. So we can keep Camden safe."

"Camden?" Colleen asked.

"My son. That's what Lucas named him, and I will make sure no one, including you, does anything to harm him."

That didn't do much to ease Colleen's alarm. "You think I was together with him on this," she concluded. "I'm your sister."

"Yes, but we haven't always seen eye to eye in the past. You refused to testify against Preston."

Colleen's alarm turned to something else, and Lucas was pretty sure that something else was anger. It flashed through her eyes. "Because as you well know, I didn't witness the crimes you said he did."

There it was. Not just her words but Colleen's tone. Yeah, there was bitterness. Maybe because Colleen had been personally involved with the man? Or maybe she'd been doing more than only IT work for him.

"Why would Darrin want you dead?" Colleen came out and asked Hailey.

Lucas hoped she wouldn't mention those files, and she didn't. Hailey only shook her head. "Is it possible he was working for Preston and that Preston left orders to have me killed?"

"No," Colleen answered. Way too fast. She was definitely in the defensive mode when it came to her former boss. "Preston wouldn't have done that."

"How do you know that?" Lucas snapped.

Colleen volleyed some annoyed glances between Hailey and him. "Because I visited Preston in jail a few times."

Lucas rolled his eyes, took out his phone. "If I call the prison, I can find out exactly how many visits you made."

Her mouth tightened. "I saw him every week. And I'm not going to apologize for that."

"You should," Lucas argued. "Because even from behind bars, Preston could have arranged for the attacks against Hailey."

"He didn't," Colleen practically yelled. It took her a moment to regain her composure, and then she shifted her gaze back to Hailey. "You always believed the worst about Preston, but I believe it was the dirty agent who set him up. The same agent who's been trying to get into this room. Probably to kill me. Maybe he's the one who wants to kill Camden and you."

That was entirely possible. "You have any proof that Agent Minton is dirty?" Lucas asked her.

"No, but since you're a lawman, you should be the one getting that proof. Because someone put me in this hospital bed, and the next time, he might succeed in putting me in the grave."

Because that was possible, too, Lucas decided it was time to have a more thorough chat with Minton. Of course, that meant Hailey spending a little more time in the room with her sister, but Lucas could chat with Minton in the doorway. That way, he could keep an eye on Hailey.

Lucas opened the door, expecting to come face-to-face with the riled agent, but Minton wasn't there. However, Josh wasn't alone. There was another man standing in front of him. A man that Lucas recognized from the research he'd done the night before.

Eric DeSalvo.

Like Minton, Eric was wearing a suit. But he sure wasn't scowling. The man was smiling. A slick kind of smile that reminded Lucas of a snake oil salesman.

"You're supposed to be at the sheriff's office for an interview," Lucas immediately reminded Eric.

"I'm on my way there, but I decided to make a detour." His smile widened. "Lucas Ryland, Texas Ranger," Eric greeted him. Obviously the man had done his research as well. "I understand you think I'm guilty of all sorts of assorted felonies."

"Are you?" Lucas growled.

"No, but I think I can help you solve this." He tipped his head to the end of the hall, where Lucas saw Minton walking away. "Arrange a plea deal for me, and I'll give you what you need to put Agent Minton behind bars."

Chapter Seven

Hailey hadn't wanted to make this trip to the Silver Creek Sheriff's Office. She'd wanted to be back at the ranch with her son. But these interviews could be critical to helping Lucas and her make sure that Camden stayed safe.

Well, there was one official interview anyway—with Eric.

But since Agent Minton had shown up, Grayson would be questioning him, as well. Of course, that didn't mean Minton would answer anything. Especially anything that could incriminate him, but maybe he would spill something that would be helpful. For that matter, maybe Eric would do the same, and this nightmare would stop right here, right now.

"They're about ready to start," Lucas said, joining her by the observation window of the interview room. He handed her a cup of much-needed coffee.

Eric was already seated at the gray metal table, an attorney on each side of him, and even though he couldn't see Hailey through the one-way glass, he occasionally looked in her direction. And he smiled again.

No doubt to unnerve her.

There was certainly no love lost between them, and after his father had been convicted, Eric had issued plenty of veiled threats to get to her. Not because he'd wanted to defend Preston. He hadn't.

Eric hadn't had much love for his father, either, but he hadn't wanted Hailey to do anything that would include him in the charges against Preston. Father and son still had plenty of business ties. Ties that Preston would have gladly continued because from all accounts, he'd wanted to protect his son.

Hailey now understood the lengths a parent would go to to protect a child. Even when that child—Eric—had done everything to distance himself from his father.

"Where's Minton?" she asked.

Lucas hitched his thumb to the hall. "In the other interview room, where Dade will question him. Let's just say he's not happy about being questioned by a *local yokel* deputy sheriff, and he's on his phone to his boss to find out if he can get out of it."

Maybe his boss would side with Grayson. And even if he didn't, perhaps they could get the information some other way.

She glanced back at Eric when he smiled at her again. "Any idea what kind of plea deal he wants?"

Lucas shook his head. "After dropping the bombshell at the hospital, he clammed up, claimed he didn't want to say anything else without his attorneys present."

That didn't surprise her. "Eric always hides behind his attorneys. So did his father. Not the same attorneys, of course. Preston would have shared, but Eric never trusted his father enough to mix his personal stuff with the family business."

Lucas stared at her. "After this, you should be able to access those files. Too bad you can't do that before Grayson talks to Eric, because there might be something he could use for leverage. Just how much jail time would Eric get with what you have?"

"Not nearly enough. It's an illegal sale of some land. He paid off some officials one county over and got the land rezoned so he could in turn sell it to one of his puppet companies. There's also a sale of confiscated weapons."

That got his attention. He moved even closer.

So close that his arm brushed against hers. It was just a slight touch, but she felt it head to toe.

"How many weapons?" he asked.

"Not nearly enough," she repeated after she gathered the breath to speak. Mercy, she had to figure out how to stop these flutters when she was around Lucas. She also had to focus since this was an important conversation. "It's a felony, but since he's got a spotless record, he might not get more than a year."

Lucas's forehead bunched up. "Yet it was enough to keep his father from coming after you."

"Preston loved him. Despite everything."

"Exactly what is *everything*?" he asked.

Because he was looking her straight in the eyes and because he was so close to her, it took Hailey a moment to realize they were still talking about Eric. And not this attraction between them.

"I don't know all the details," Hailey explained, "but Preston was a widower since Eric was a little boy, and Eric always blamed his father for his mother's death."

"Was Preston to blame?"

"I don't know, but she did die in a car accident. The cops did investigate it. Nothing concrete turned up, though."

Lucas made a sound, one of skepticism. A

sound that Hailey totally understood. "Three car wrecks, and I know mine wasn't an accident," she said. "Perhaps the others weren't, either."

"You think Colleen's telling the truth about that? About any of this?" he asked.

Hailey drew in a long breath. "I want to believe her. But things have sometimes been—well—tense between us. She was three when her father married my mother, and I think once I was born a couple of years later, she thought our parents doted on me more than her. And maybe they did when I was little. Then our mother died of breast cancer, and my father ended up abandoning us. Colleen blamed me for that, too."

She stopped and realized she'd never told anyone that. "Sorry," Hailey said. "Didn't mean to dump all of that on you."

"No. I wanted to hear it because it's motive. People have certainly killed for a lot less, and coupled with her disapproval over you testifying against Preston, maybe Colleen decided she'd had enough."

That turned Hailey's stomach. Because *enough* nearly cost her Camden.

"What happened to Colleen and you after your father left?" Lucas continued.

"Foster care. That's when we got closer. I think because we only had each other."

And now Colleen might be trying to kill her. Of course, her sister wasn't their main suspect. That person was sitting on the other side of the observation mirror, and Eric smiled again when Grayson finally came into the room.

Lucas reached over to turn on the audio so they could hear the interview, and again his arm brushed against hers. The other time he hadn't noticed. Or at least, he'd pretended not to notice. But this time their gazes met.

And held.

He mumbled some profanity and looked away. "This isn't going to happen," he said, but she wasn't sure if he was trying to convince her or himself.

No way did he want to get involved with her. She totally understood that, but the attraction was undeniable. The heat was still just as strong as it had been the night she'd gone to his bed. Thankfully she didn't have to keep remembering it, because Grayson got her attention when he spoke.

"Tell me about this plea deal you want," Grayson demanded.

Eric looked directly into the mirror. "I've heard that Hailey might have something she believes could be incriminating about me. It'll be all fake, of course, but I need the chance to clear my name."

"You said you thought that Eric didn't know about those computer files," Lucas reminded her.

"I didn't think he did. The only one I personally told was Preston."

Lucas stayed quiet a couple of seconds. "Is it possible Preston told Colleen?"

Hailey sighed. Nodded. Yes, it was possible. "But why would Colleen have told Eric?"

Lucas didn't get a chance to answer because Grayson continued. "What kind of incriminating info?" Grayson pressed. He knew all about the computer files they'd soon be able to access, but he no doubt wanted to hear Eric's take on this.

"I'm not positive, but I think it's supposed to be about illegal arms. It could be anything since it's fake."

Grayson just stared at him. "And you think Hailey manufactured this?"

Eric shrugged. "Probably not her, but my father could have."

"From everything I've heard, your father cared about you. In fact, I heard he'd do pretty much anything to prevent you from going to jail."

"That's what he wanted everyone to believe, but as a lawman, you certainly know what he was capable of. It's not much of a stretch to think he'd come up with something to keep me in line."

Oh, mercy. Was it false evidence? "It looked real," she said to Lucas. "And besides, if it were fake, why wouldn't Preston have sent someone after me? He hated me for testifying against him."

"Maybe even Preston didn't have the stomach for murdering a woman in a coma. Still... the latest attacks didn't happen until after he was dead."

True. And that led them right back to Eric.

"All right," Grayson continued. "You want a look at these so-called files. What are you offering in exchange?"

"Some files of my own," Eric said without hesitation. "They won't be admissible in court, but they're recordings that my father made when people visited his office."

Judging from Eric's smug look, there was something critical on the recordings. Judging from Grayson's scowl, he wasn't pleased about it.

"Any reason you didn't turn these recordings over to the authorities when the investigation was going on?" Grayson snapped.

Eric's smug look went up a notch. "Because I only recently found them. Yesterday, in fact."

Hailey groaned. He was lying. He'd probably had them all along. But why had he held on to them?

"Eric's up to something," Hailey mumbled.

Lucas made a sound of agreement, but before he could say anything, the door to the observation room opened, and she saw Dade and Minton standing there.

"I've played along with this fiasco long enough," Minton snarled. "I'm an FBI agent and won't be treated like this."

"Let me guess," Lucas said to his cousin. "The interview went well." His voice dripped with sarcasm.

"No, it didn't." Minton's tone was full of sarcasm, too. "I don't know anything that can help you end whatever the hell's happening to Hailey. And I won't know until you tell me everything that's going on." He glanced at the mirror. "Including what's going on with that piece of slime."

Hailey wanted to tune Minton out and focus on Eric's conversation, but Grayson, the lawyers and the DA had moved on to the details of the plea deal, and from what Hailey could tell, Eric was asking for immunity from prosecution.

Which meant there was likely something incriminating him on those recordings or in the files Hailey had.

Hailey hadn't intended to bring up anything

to Minton about what Eric had just said, but Lucas obviously had something different in mind.

"Eric claims he has recordings that he got from his father's office," Lucas tossed out there. "He's working out a plea deal now."

And Hailey soon knew why Lucas had done that. He pinned his attention to Minton, clearly looking for a reaction.

He got one.

Minton charged toward the window to have a closer look. "Any recordings come under the jurisdiction of the FBI."

Lucas huffed. "You seem to keep forgetting that this isn't an FBI matter. The recordings could be evidence in the recent attacks against Hailey. Attacks that happened right here in Silver Creek." He glanced at Dade. "Did anyone here in the sheriff's office request FBI assistance? Because that's the only way Minton could be involved in this."

Dade pretended to think about that. "Nope. No one here made a request like that. Grayson said if we needed help, we'd call in the Rangers. Of course, we won't have to call very loud since a Texas Ranger is standing right here in this room."

Minton's mouth tightened, but instead of verbal fire at any of the men, he turned toward

Hailey. "I'm trying to keep you and your son alive." He nodded toward Eric. "You'll need all the help you can get with that piece of slime. He's dangerous. That's why you should give me copies of anything you have on him."

Lucas's huff was even louder this time. "This conversation is over." And he took Hailey by the arm and maneuvered her around Minton and Dade.

"It's not over," Minton insisted. "One way or another, I will get the evidence you have."

It sounded like a threat. Worse, it felt like one.

Hailey reminded herself that Minton could just be focused on the job, but if he was the dirty agent Preston had on his payroll, then she had two snakes to watch out for—Eric and Minton.

"I'll take you back to the ranch," Lucas said once they were out of earshot of Minton. "We'll wait there until you can get into the files. Maybe by then Grayson will have worked out something with Eric."

They went to the front where Lucas had left the cruiser, but before they reached the door, his phone buzzed. Hailey saw Josh's name on the screen. Since he was at the hospital, she instantly got a bad feeling.

Lucas obviously did, too, because he belted out some profanity under his breath. "A problem?" Lucas greeted his cousin.

"Yeah. Please tell me we have something to hold Colleen. Because if not, she's about to leave the hospital."

Hailey released the breath she'd been holding. She'd braced herself for something worse, like an attack. "Did the doctor say it was okay for her to go?"

"No. But she's leaving anyway unless we've got grounds to hold her."

"She was on the surveillance tape with a hit man," Hailey reminded Lucas.

But Lucas shook his head. "Not enough since she had an explanation for that, and there's no proof that she knew who he was. Can Colleen hear me talking right now?" he asked Josh.

"No," Josh repeated. "She's in her room getting dressed, and I'm in the hall."

"Good. Then let her leave, but I want a tail on her. Tell me where she goes and who she sees. Because if she's behind this, she might try to meet with her hired thugs."

True. Hailey hated to think Colleen would do that, but this might be a way to be sure.

"Will do," Josh said. "Hold on while I send a text to the reserve deputy who's in the parking lot. He's dressed in plain clothes."

Maybe Colleen wouldn't notice the man and would do whatever it was she was setting out to do. Part of Hailey wished, though, that her sister had had no part in any of this.

"Colleen's coming out of her room now," Josh added a moment later.

Josh said something else, something that Hailey didn't catch. Ditto for whatever her sister said to the deputy.

"Colleen just handed me a note that I'm supposed to give to Hailey," Josh finally explained.

"A note?" Hailey asked. "Why didn't she just talk to me?"

"Don't know. You want me to unfold it and read it to you?"

"Yes," she answered as fast as she could.

Hailey heard the rustling around on Josh's end, and a moment later he mumbled some of the same profanity that Lucas had just used. "It says, 'I'm sorry, Hailey. I know you'll never understand, but I did what I had to do.'"

Chapter Eight

"I did what I had to do."

Lucas hoped Colleen was referring to checking herself out of the hospital, but he had a bad feeling in the pit of his stomach.

It certainly hadn't helped when Colleen had managed to ditch the tail they had on her. Now she was in the wind. Could have been anywhere. Heck, she could have been out there planning another attack. Colleen had a lot of questions to answer, but first they had to find her and somehow force her to tell them the truth.

Of course, in addition to Colleen, Lucas had plenty of other things adding to that bad feeling. Minton, Eric.

And Hailey.

Hailey, though, was a bad feeling of a different kind.

Once again, he had no choice but to take her to his house at the ranch. It was either that or spend more time at the sheriff's office, and neither of them wanted that. In fact, Hailey had jumped to say yes when he suggested they go.

Hailey had *jumped* yet again when they'd arrived home and Tillie had offered to show her how to give Camden his bottle. Now Lucas was supervising that while he waited for updates on both the plea deal and Colleen.

"He really is a little miracle," Hailey said, smiling at Camden while she burped him.

Of course, Hailey was in heaven over doing something as simple as feeding and burping their son. "You might not call him a miracle when he wakes up every three hours," Lucas joked, because he thought they could use some levity.

At least, he could use it, anyway. His muscles were knotted so tight that his back and shoulders were hurting.

Hailey smiled, and he got a knot of a different kind. This one in his stomach. He remembered that smile. It was one of the first things that had attracted him to her, and even now it stalled his breath in his chest. Then she chuckled when Camden let out a burp that sounded as if it'd come from a grown man drinking beer. Lucas didn't join her on the chuckling, but he'd had the same reaction the first couple of times it had happened.

His phone dinged with a text from Josh.

Lucas glanced at his watch. "You should be able to get into the storage cloud to retrieve those files." That would get his mind off her smile and back to what he should have been focusing on.

She nodded, her forehead bunching up. Obviously she didn't want to let go of the baby just yet, but Lucas needed to see exactly what Hailey had against Eric.

Hailey kissed Camden, and she waited for Tillie to come and take the baby before she got up from the chair. She made her way to Lucas's office just up the hall. It seemed as if each hour she was walking a little better, but she still caught onto the wall to steady herself.

And she also caught onto him when she eased into the chair.

"Sorry," she said. No doubt because she felt his muscles tense. "I know it bothers you for me to touch you."

Yeah, it did. But not in the way she was thinking. It bothered him because it reminded him of things he shouldn't have been remembering. Instead of mentioning that, though, Lucas just motioned for her to get busy on the laptop.

She nodded, looked disappointed that he hadn't addressed the elephant in the room—

the attraction. Something he had no plans to address.

"It'll take a couple of minutes for me to get through the passwords and security questions," she said just as his phone rang.

Since it was Grayson's name on the screen and no doubt a call about the investigation, Lucas answered it on speaker. That way Hailey wouldn't have to lean too close to him to hear.

"We worked out a plea deal with Eric," Grayson said. "A limited one for both of us. He'll get immunity only if there's something of evidentiary value on the recordings. The second condition is that the immunity will cover only one criminal count. A count that doesn't include murder or accessory to murder."

Lucas looked at Hailey. "Any chance of Eric having murdered someone?"

"Not that I know of," she answered. "From what I learned, the DeSalvo family crimes seemed to be limited to money laundering and the sale of illegal arms. Of course, it's possible someone was killed during those deals, but the deals I had knowledge of were mainly Preston's, not Eric's."

That didn't mean Eric didn't have any side deals of his own. But then, if he had, there was no way the man would give Grayson evidence to incriminate himself for murder.

"What did you mean about the deal being limited for both Eric and you?" Hailey wanted to know.

"The recordings are on old compact disks, and Preston set it up so they can't be copied. Eric wants the disks to stay here in the sheriff's office, and that means I'll have to tie up some manpower to listen to them."

Eric had probably added that into the deal to make sure Minton and the FBI didn't get their hands on them. Or maybe Eric had another reason for doing that.

"Did Eric give you any idea what was on the recordings?" Lucas asked Grayson.

"He says he hasn't listened to them all. Which I find hard to believe."

So did Lucas. Eric didn't seem like the sort to shoot himself in the foot by handing over anything that could be connected to him beyond the limits of the plea deal. Still, there might be something that Eric had missed.

"But what Eric did say," Grayson went on, "was that there are dozens of recorded conversations with his father and his business associates. Of course, he didn't get permission from any of these people. But there are names, he claims, that we can use to make some arrests if we can link those names to the crimes."

Yeah, because the recordings themselves

probably wouldn't be admissible in court since Preston didn't get prior consent from at least one of the people he was recording. Then there was the problem of the tapes being in the hands of one of their suspects, one who could have doctored the conversations.

"I'll call you as soon as we have the recordings. Let me know what you find out from Hailey's files," Grayson added before he ended the call.

Lucas put away his phone and watched as Hailey accessed the site. Thankfully her fingers were working better than her legs. She had no trouble typing.

No trouble cursing, either.

That bad feeling in his stomach went up a couple of notches.

"The files are gone?" Lucas concluded, but he hoped he was wrong.

Hailey didn't answer him. She kept mumbling profanity. Kept searching through the storage cloud. Even though Lucas was far from a computer expert, he could see that all the files were empty.

Except one.

Hailey clicked on it, and when Lucas saw what was there, he was the one cursing. Not files to incriminate Eric. There was just a single document with one sentence written on it.

I did what I had to do.

It was the exact wording of the note Colleen had left with Josh, but in this case it didn't make sense.

"Why would Colleen want these files deleted?" Lucas asked. "From what I can tell, Colleen despises Eric."

Hailey groaned, obviously still dealing with the bombshell of what her sister had done. Or else what someone wanted them to believe Colleen had done.

"She does," Hailey confirmed. But then she shook her head. "Or maybe that was all a pretense. I just don't know anymore."

Another groan, and she buried her face in her hands for a couple of seconds. When she lowered them, Lucas spotted the tears in her eyes.

Oh, man. Not tears. Not now. He was already feeling raw and exhausted, and he was a sucker for a woman's tears. Especially this woman. Because this was quickly turning into a very bad day for Hailey and this investigation.

She stood and looked around as if trying to decide what to do, but Lucas could see that there wasn't much fight left in her. "Colleen must hate me to side with a snake like Eric."

"Maybe she didn't have a choice. Maybe Eric

has some dirt on her. Something that would send her to jail."

The tears continued. "Yes, but she knows those files are meant to protect Camden and me from Eric. Or from any of Preston's thugs who might be out there ready to carry out their late boss's dying wish to see me dead."

She was right. And Lucas had had enough of the tears. Before he could talk himself out of it, he reached out and pulled her into his arms. Of course, Hailey had been in his arms since she'd come out of the coma. It'd been necessary to keep her from falling.

This was different.

Lucas could feel it. And Hailey could feel it, too. She didn't go stiff as she had the other times they'd touched in the past twenty-four hours. She sort of melted against him.

"I'm just so scared," she admitted. "Not for me but for Camden and you. For your family."

"No one is going to hurt Camden or my family," he assured her. Not that he was in a position to give that kind of assurance. Not with hired guns after them. Still, those hired guns would have to get past him, and since he was protecting his son, Lucas had no intention of making that easy for them.

Hailey looked up at him at the exact moment he looked down at her. Lucas silently said more of that profanity. He was so not ready for this. Well, his mind and heart weren't, anyway, but the rest of him seemed to think it was a good idea to kiss her or something.

Especially *something*.

The heat came. Memories, too. Vivid memories of Hailey naked and beneath him in his bed. The very bed that was just up the hall.

She didn't look away from him, and hell, he didn't look away, either. They just stood there with all those bad thoughts running through his head. Lucas was within a fraction of a second of acting on those bad thoughts by kissing her, but Hailey cleared her throat and stepped back.

"I'm sorry," Hailey said, rubbing her forehead and dodging his gaze. "I know that makes things worse."

It did, and Lucas didn't want her to clarify that. Or talk about it. Hell, he just wanted to concentrate on anything but this ache that was begging him to have sex with her right here, right now.

"You should try to call Colleen and ask her about this," he managed to say, and he handed her his phone.

Focus. He needed to deal with the problems of the investigation and not create new problems by having his body go rock hard with thoughts of Hailey.

She nodded. "I'm not sure if Colleen still has the same number. Until I came out of the coma, I hadn't been in touch with her since Preston's trial, and that was over eighteen months ago."

It was a long shot, but it was one that paid off. In a way. Colleen didn't answer, but when her voice mail greeting kicked in, Hailey and he got verification that her sister had kept the old number.

"Call me ASAP," Hailey said when she left the message, and there was a definite urgency in her tone.

But whether Colleen would phone her back was a different matter. After all, even though she'd been injured in that car accident, Colleen had still managed to elude the reserve deputy. Something Lucas wished he'd handled differently. He should have requested one of the regular deputies to follow her.

Hailey sank back down onto the chair and gave a heavy sigh. At least she wasn't crying, but this was obviously getting to her. Or rather, it was, until she looked up at him again, and there was something in her eyes. Not attraction this time.

"What if Colleen and Eric believe I have hard copies of everything that was in the online storage?" she asked.

It didn't take long, only a few seconds, for

Lucas to figure out where this was going. And he shook his head. "You're talking about setting a trap. Definitely not a good idea, because it could send those hired killers after you again."

"The hired killers will come no matter what. I'm not sure why, but obviously the person behind this sees me as a threat. Or maybe the things that I know are what he or she considers the threat."

That was true, and it didn't rule out any of their suspects. Minton could want anything destroyed that could link him to being a dirty agent. Eric could be trying to save his butt from going to jail. And Colleen? Well, Lucas still didn't know why she was seemingly playing on Eric's side in this, but it was obvious she didn't want her sister to have any incriminating evidence about the man.

Or maybe the information in the file incriminated someone else? Like Colleen herself?

Too bad they didn't have the real files to examine.

"Just think this through," Hailey pressed. "We could leak that the computer files have been erased and that I'm getting the hard copies to give to Grayson. We could say that I'm getting them from a safe deposit box or something."

Lucas huffed. It would still put Hailey in immediate danger. Unless…

"Maybe we could get a cop to go in posing as you," Lucas said. "There's a reserve deputy, Kara Duggan, who has a similar height and build. We could arrange for there to be eyes on her and give her plenty of backup." But then he paused. "Of course, the gunmen might be expecting a trap and come here after you."

She pressed her lips together a moment. Clearly this thought had already occurred to her, but then Hailey's gaze drifted in the direction of the nursery. If the gunmen came here, Camden would be in danger.

"How about you and I go to the sheriff's office and then leak the info?" she suggested. "That way, if they do smell a trap, they'll go after me there and not come to the ranch."

Lucas went through all the things that could go wrong. And with hired killers, there was plenty that could go wrong.

"You know that none of our suspects will go after the decoy, right?" he reminded her. "He or she will send a lackey."

Hailey nodded. "But if we have a lackey—alive—we might be able to find out who hired him."

True. Once they had the hired thug's name, then they could search for a paper trail or maybe work out a plea deal. Still, it wasn't without huge risks.

"You're sure you want to do this?" Lucas asked.

"I'm sure," Hailey said without hesitation.

Lucas hesitated, but he knew this was the only straw they had a chance to grab right now. He took out his phone, but it rang before he could call Grayson to set all of this up.

Dade's name popped up on the screen. "We got the recordings from Eric," Dade told Lucas. "They're actual disks. Dozens of them. He flagged one that we should listen to first. It's a conversation between Preston and Colleen." He paused. "I really think Hailey should hear what her sister had to say. Then we can figure out what we need to do."

Chapter Nine

Hailey didn't know what she was dreading more—this return trip to the sheriff's office to hear the recorded conversation that Dade had said she'd definitely want to hear, or leaving Camden.

Still, it was necessary. Not just for the recordings but also because they needed to work out the final details for the trap to lure out whoever was behind this. She hated that the reserve deputy would be in possible danger, but Hailey was hoping that Lucas would be able to set it all up so they could minimize the risks.

"Maybe this won't take long," Lucas said as they got into the cruiser.

They weren't alone. Josh and one of the armed ranch hands, Avery Joyner, were with them. Josh was behind the wheel with Avery riding shotgun. Lucas and she took the backseat.

"And I'm still not sure this is a good idea," Lucas added.

She'd lost count how many times he'd said a variation of that, and Hailey agreed with him. She wasn't sure it was a good idea, either, but at the moment they didn't have a lot of options as to how to put an end to the danger. Plus, she really did want to listen to those recordings. Of course, she could have had Dade play the conversations for her over the phone, but from the sound of it, there'd need to be some follow-up action when it came to her sister.

"Colleen or Preston must have said something bad for Dade to have called," Hailey remarked.

Lucas made a sound of agreement, but what he didn't do was take his attention off their surroundings. Like Avery and Josh, his gaze was firing all around them, watching for anyone who might attack them. "Not a surprise, though. After all, she's the one who likely deleted those computer files."

True. But there was something about it that didn't feel right. People with solid computer skills could have hacked their way in and then set up her sister to take the blame.

"What the hell?" Josh mumbled, and he slowed the cruiser.

Hailey followed his gaze to the end of the

road, where someone had parked a black car. The road was barely a few yards off Ryland land, which was probably why the security system hadn't detected it, but there were also two ranch hands armed with rifles. They weren't pointing the rifles at their visitor, but Hailey figured they would if he tried to get on the ranch road.

"You know that man?" Avery asked Lucas.

And that's when Hailey spotted Minton stepping from the car.

"Yeah," Lucas answered. "That's FBI Agent Brian Minton."

Both Lucas and she groaned. She definitely didn't want to deal with the agent today. Especially since he was one of their suspects. But from the way Minton had parked, they wouldn't be able to get around him without speaking to the man. Judging from the way Lucas was cursing, the *speaking* wouldn't be friendly.

"Wait here, and I'll see what he wants," Lucas said to Hailey. He drew his gun, reached for the door but then glanced back at her. "And I mean it about waiting inside the cruiser. If Minton's behind the attacks, he could have snipers in the area."

That caused her heart to jump to her throat, and Hailey caught onto his arm. "If there are possible snipers, it's too risky for you to go out there."

"I won't be long," Lucas insisted, as if that made everything okay. Hailey wanted to remind him that it took only a split second for someone to gun him down, but he was out of the cruiser before she could even gather her breath.

Josh opened his door, as well. So did Avery. And they drew their guns while continuing to watch around them. Hailey tried to do the same, but it was hard not to focus on Minton and Lucas. Thankfully, with the front doors open, she could hear Minton when he *greeted* Lucas.

"These men wouldn't let me onto the ranch," Minton complained.

"Because they're smart and following orders. *My* orders. No one's getting onto the ranch unless you live or work here. Neither applies to you."

In addition to hearing them well enough, Hailey had no trouble seeing Minton's steely expression. "We're fellow peace officers. You'd think we could cooperate long enough to bring someone to justice. Especially since that someone is obviously after Hailey and now you since you're trying to protect her. They'll kill you to get to her."

"Cooperate? Right. You and I have a different notion about what that means. You want me to give this investigation to the FBI, and it's not mine to give. Sheriff Grayson Ryland is in charge."

"Well, he shouldn't be," Minton snapped. Every muscle in his face was tight, but he said something under his breath. Something she didn't catch. And then it appeared he was trying to rein in his temper. "I just need the information, that's all. I need to know what Hailey has. Eric, too. Especially Eric, because he could have altered those recordings." Minton paused. "I think Eric's trying to set me up."

"And how and why would he do that?" Lucas asked.

"I'm investigating him, and I think I'm close to giving him a dose of the justice he deserves. He'd obviously do anything to stop me, and that includes doctoring the tapes that he claims he just found. Eric's got the money and resources to do something like that."

Interesting. Maybe Minton was trying to do some damage control beforehand just in case there was anything in those conversations about him.

"Did you and Preston have conversations in his office?" Lucas pressed. He was still keeping watch around them, and while Hailey knew this chat could be important, she didn't want Lucas out there any longer.

Minton nodded. "A couple of them, in fact. Remember, I was investigating both Eric and him, and I interviewed Preston. Anything I said could be altered or taken out of context, and I just don't want my name sullied because of a snake like Eric."

"I get that, but it still doesn't mean you can listen to the recordings. Eric worked out a plea deal, and we have to abide by that." Lucas glanced around again. "If you want to keep up this little chat, then call the sheriff's office and make an appointment." With that, he headed back to the cruiser.

Obviously Minton didn't like being dismissed that way, because the flash of anger returned on his face. "Not cooperating with me is a huge mistake," the agent snarled, and he, too, turned back toward his car.

He didn't get far.

Because a shot slammed through the air and smashed right into the front end of Minton's car.

HELL.

Lucas had known right from the start that something like this could happen, but he'd hoped he would get lucky. Apparently not, though.

He was still a few yards from the cruiser and started to run so he could dive in, but the next shot stopped him. It didn't go toward Minton's car but right at Lucas. He had to drop to the ground, and it wasn't a second too soon.

Because if Lucas hadn't, the next shot would have hit him.

"Get in!" Hailey yelled.

He had no trouble hearing her and the fear in her voice, but Lucas hoped like the devil that she was staying down. The windows in the cruiser were bullet-resistant. That didn't mean, though, that these shots wouldn't eventually tear their way through the glass and reach her.

Another shot came.

This one landed near Minton again, and like Lucas, the agent had no choice but to go to the ground and use his car as cover. The ranch hands outside took cover, as well. They scrambled into the ditch.

Good.

Lucas didn't want them in the line of fire, but he also needed the attack to stop. Because they weren't the only ones in danger. Anyone else on the ranch could be hit if this idiot trying to kill them had a long enough range.

Judging from the sound of the shots, they were coming from a heavily treed area across the road. The oaks were huge there and would make the perfect catbird seat for a sniper. But that wasn't all that Lucas realized. There was more than one gunman.

"Can you see who's shooting?" Minton called out to him.

"No. But I think they're at your eleven and one o'clock."

Lucas only hoped there weren't more, but considering the other attacks, there was no telling how many the sick person behind this had sent after them.

The two gunmen were clearly working together to keep all five of them pinned down while also keeping watch on the cruiser. When Josh tried to open the door, no doubt to return fire, one of the gunmen sent a bullet his way. Definitely not good because it didn't stop with just one shot. A barrage of bullets went into the cruiser, each of them with the possibility of being deadly.

Lucas had to do something *now*.

"Minton, somehow you need to get in your car and move it," Lucas ordered.

Because until he did that, they wouldn't be able to move the cruiser forward and get the heck out of there. There was no way Lucas wanted to go in reverse and have these hired guns just follow them onto the ranch.

Minton did try to move. He made it a few

inches before the shots turned in his direction, and he had to scramble to the ground again.

By now, someone had called for backup, and even though there were several of his lawmen cousins on the grounds, they wouldn't be able to get to them right now without putting themselves in grave danger.

The shots shifted again. Some went in the direction of the ditch. No doubt because Avery had tried to fire. Since the hands were armed with rifles, they would stand a better chance of putting an end to this than Lucas would with his handgun. It was obvious, though, that the thugs weren't going to give the men a chance to shoot.

Lucas glanced over at the cruiser to make sure Hailey was staying put. She wasn't. She was by the door nearest him, and she was opening it as wide as it would go. Of course, that caused the gunmen to fire at her.

"Get down!" Lucas told her.

He didn't want her risking her life, but he was thankful about the door maneuver. It would make it easier for him to get back into the cruiser if he could just get a break from the gunmen. Even then, though, he'd still need Minton to get the devil out of the way.

"I'll create a diversion," Lucas said to Minton. He didn't shout and hoped his voice didn't carry so the gunmen would hear him. "When they start shooting at me, get to your car."

Minton nodded. Lucas had to admit that the man looked just as concerned about this as Lucas was. Maybe that meant Minton wasn't a dirty agent after all. But then, this could all be a ruse to make him look innocent, especially since no one had actually been shot. The gunmen would have had ample opportunity to do that when Minton and he had been talking out in the open.

Anything that Lucas did at this point was a risk, but doing nothing was even riskier, so he got into position the way a sprinter would at the start line, and after saying a quick prayer, he bolted toward the cruiser.

"No!" Hailey shouted when Lucas started moving.

But he was already doing that diversion that he hoped would work. It did. The shots started coming right at him, each of them smacking into the ground and kicking up bits of asphalt right at him. Still, Lucas didn't stop. He barreled to the cruiser and jumped inside.

"You shouldn't have done that," Hailey cried out. She grabbed him and pulled him into her arms.

Lucas could feel her shaking. Could feel the relief, too. Relief he understood because he was feeling it as well. But he couldn't think about that right now. Instead, using the cruiser door for cover, he took aim and started shooting in the direction of those gunmen. They were perhaps out of range, but it might distract them enough to buy Minton a little time.

Avery joined Lucas, and both of them fired. For the first time since this attack had begun, the gunmen stopped shooting. It was just enough time for Minton to dart around to the side of his car and get in.

"Put on your seat belt," Lucas told Hailey.

He didn't have to tell Josh to get ready to move because his cousin had already put the cruiser in gear. Thankfully it didn't take long for Minton to start his car engine, and as soon as he'd done that, he hit the accelerator.

Josh did the same.

Minton sped out onto the main road, turning toward town. The majority of the bullets followed him, slamming into the back of his car. But some of the shots came at the cruiser, too.

"Don't go the same direction as Minton," Lucas instructed Josh.

His cousin didn't question that, probably because he already knew that Lucas considered Minton a suspect. Josh went in the opposite direction. That would also get them to town. Eventually. But it was a longer route. Still, as long as it got them out of the path of those shots, Lucas didn't mind the extra miles.

Well, provided he could keep Hailey safe by going that extra distance. Lucas didn't want to be near Minton, but he also hoped they weren't heading straight for another attack.

"I've already called Mason," Josh explained. "He heard the shots and was already putting the ranch on lockdown. Grayson's sending someone to find those snipers."

Lucas figured they wouldn't be easy to find. They'd probably had a darn good escape route mapped out before either of them ever pulled their triggers. Still, that didn't mean they wouldn't leave some kind of evidence behind.

"Is anyone following us?" Avery asked, looking around.

Lucas was looking, as well, but he didn't see anyone. Not at first, anyway. And then, just ahead, he spotted the black SUV that had pulled into an old ranch trail. Josh no doubt saw it, as well, because he muttered some profanity under his breath.

No way could it be the shooters because they wouldn't have had time to leave those trees and make it to this point. But Lucas doubted that it was a coincidence that someone happened to be on this rural stretch of the road at the same time someone had been trying to kill them.

"Turn around," Lucas said to Josh. He kept his attention pinned to the vehicle while he pushed Hailey down onto the seat. "Go back in the other direction."

It was dangerous, but he didn't want to risk driving past that SUV in case someone started shooting at them again. Best to get Hailey to safety, and then he could have the deputies go on the search for the SUV.

"Don't stop by the ranch," Lucas added. "Just keep driving to the sheriff's office."

Josh hit the brakes, and even though the road was barely wide enough to do a U-turn, his cousin managed it by using the gravel shoulder of the road. He got the cruiser headed in the other direction. But not before Lucas caught a glimpse of the people inside the SUV.

"No," Hailey said under her breath. And Lucas knew from her tone and her gasp that she'd seen them, too.

There was a man behind the wheel. Someone that Lucas didn't recognize, but he sure as heck knew the person in the front passenger seat.

Colleen.

Chapter Ten

One minute Hailey felt numb from the spent adrenaline, but the next minute she wanted to scream. Yet another attack could have killed them.

Attacks perhaps orchestrated by her own sister.

It turned her stomach to relive the image of Colleen in that SUV. Less than a half mile from those snipers at the ranch. Had she been sitting there, staying close to her hired thugs? Because she certainly didn't look like a hostage.

From the glimpse that Hailey had gotten of her, she'd seen no restraints on Colleen, but her sister had looked surprised to see her. Maybe because Colleen had figured they'd be heading toward town and not her direction.

The one good thing in all of this was that Camden and the rest of the people at the ranch were safe. Their attackers hadn't tried to get onto the grounds to continue their rampage there. Even more, Mason had sent additional armed ranch hands to guard Lucas's house. Of course, they wouldn't be able to go outside, but that was better than putting themselves in harm's way.

"Are you okay?" Lucas asked her.

Hailey didn't even try to pretend she was. She just shook her head and hoped the truth didn't worry him too much. There was already enough worry on his face without her adding more.

Josh pulled to a stop directly in front of the sheriff's office, and Lucas quickly ushered her in. She'd already prepared herself that Minton would be there, and he was. He was also glaring at them.

"I blame you two for this," Minton snapped. "I could have been killed because of you."

Lucas returned the glare. "How do you figure that?"

"You should have already called in the FBI on this. Obviously this is too big an investigation for the locals to handle."

Now that got Grayson glaring, but it was Lucas who took up the argument with Minton.

"And by calling in the FBI, you mean *you*?" Lucas challenged the man. He huffed. "I didn't have a lot of reasons to trust you before this latest fiasco, and this didn't improve things."

"You think I had something to do with this?" Minton howled. He didn't wait for Lucas to answer. "I didn't, and because you're so stubborn about handling this yourself, you put Hailey right back in danger. Is that what you want, huh?"

"I've had enough of him," Hailey managed to whisper. She was barely hanging on by a thread, and she needed a moment to compose herself. Maybe during those moments she'd figure out how to put an end to all of this.

That's all she had to say to Lucas to get him moving. He still had his arm around her waist from when he'd ushered her in from the cruiser, and now he got her moving toward the hall, heading to the break room.

"I'm sorry," she added. "I should have just stood up to him—"

"No, and we shouldn't have stayed in the squad room for as long as we did. It could have been a ploy to keep us near the windows so that the snipers can finish us off."

Mercy. She hadn't even considered that, but she should have. She needed to be thinking clearer because the stakes were sky-high.

"I need to call Colleen again," she said, figuring that Lucas would hand her his phone to do that.

He didn't. He took her into the break room,

had her sit on the sofa. "Grayson can talk to Colleen. In fact, he'll bring her in for questioning."

Yes, because her sister was more than just a person of interest. She'd been in the vicinity of a crime scene and had likely deleted those storage files. Grayson no doubt had lots of questions for her. Anything Colleen said at this point should be part of the official investigation. Still, Hailey needed to hear what her sister had to say, and if Grayson couldn't get her in soon, then she'd try again to call her.

Lucas handed her a bottle of water that he took from the fridge. "This will have to do for now, but you probably could use something stronger."

She could indeed use it. And she got it when Lucas dropped down next to her and pulled her into his arms. It was such an unexpected gesture that Hailey went stiff for a moment. Lucas noticed, too.

He eased back a little, glanced down at her. "I know. This isn't a smart thing for me to be doing, but you look ready to drop."

"I am," she admitted. "And you're right about it not being a smart thing."

It brought back the memories of when they'd been lovers, and Hailey didn't have the energy to fend off those old images. Or the heat, which wasn't old at all. Anytime she was around Lucas, that heat flared up with a vengeance. Now was no different.

"I'm also scared," she admitted. "For Camden. For you. For all of us."

He didn't try to dismiss those fears. He couldn't. Because they were real. The danger just kept coming at them.

Lucas made a sound of agreement and eased his hold on her a little. Hailey was certain he would just pull away. But he didn't. He stayed there right next to her, and he slowly turned his head to look at her again. Since she was already looking at him, their gazes met. Held.

The air was suddenly so still it felt as if everything was holding its breath, waiting. Hailey certainly was. She had no idea where Lucas was going to take this, but she knew what she wanted.

She wanted him.

Hailey saw that want in Lucas's eyes. Saw the storm that was brewing there, too. He hadn't forgiven her for what she'd done. Probably didn't completely trust her, either, but that didn't stop this attraction.

He cursed. His voice hardly had any sound. And she saw the storm get much stronger as he lowered his head and touched his mouth to hers. It was barely a kiss, but it caused that fire inside her to blaze out of control. A simple kiss from Lucas could do that.

And then he did more. Much, much more. His mouth came to hers again, and this time it was for more than just a touch. He kissed her. Really kissed her.

His taste was a reminder of all those memories and images she'd been battling since she'd come out of the coma. A battle she was losing because the memories came flooding back and mixed with this new firestorm that the kiss was creating.

A sound rumbled in his chest. Definitely not one of agreement this time. It was one of protest and a reminder of a different sort. He didn't want to be doing this, but like her, he seemed helpless to stop it.

The kiss lingered on a moment. Then two. And just when Hailey was ready to pull him even closer Lucas stopped.

"I think I've complicated things enough for one day," he grumbled.

That made her smile even though there wasn't anything to smile about. What he'd said was the truth. The kiss had complicated things. Heck, being together upped the complications, as well, but until they found a way to put an end to the danger, they were joined at the hip.

And afterward…well, Hailey wasn't ready

to go there just yet, though she knew a future without danger also meant a future in which Lucas and she had to work out a custody arrangement for Camden.

There was a knock at the door, and a moment later Grayson opened it. He stared at them, and even though he didn't say anything about how close they were sitting, he probably noticed that they looked as if they'd just been doing something they shouldn't have been doing.

"Everything okay?" Grayson asked.

"I was about to ask you the same thing." Lucas got to his feet. "Bad news?"

Grayson lifted his shoulder. "Josh filled me in on the details of the attack. Two of the deputies just arrived in the area where those snipers were. They're not there, of course, but there are tire tracks. It's a long shot, but CSI might be able to get a match from them if they were driving a custom vehicle. The gunmen might have left prints or trace evidence behind as well."

That seemed like such a long shot, but everything was at this point. "What about the black SUV?" Hailey asked.

Grayson shook his head. "No sign of it, either. I don't guess either of you got the license plate numbers?"

"No," Lucas and she said in unison.

Hailey added a sigh. Again, she wasn't thinking straight. The shock of seeing her sister had prevented her from looking at the plates. Plus, Josh had been so fast at turning the cruiser around that she'd barely managed a glimpse of Colleen, much less any specifics about the SUV.

"Any luck getting in touch with my sister?" Hailey wanted to know.

"No. I've left her a message, and San Antonio PD will go out to her place and see if she's there."

She wouldn't be. In fact, Colleen was likely on the run right now, and there was no telling when she'd surface.

"Minton finally left," Grayson went on. "But we haven't seen the last of him."

"No, we haven't," Lucas agreed. "Either he's the most persistent FBI agent in the state or else he's dirty."

Yes, too bad they didn't know which. Because if Minton was clean, then he might truly be able to help them with this investigation.

"I know you wanted to lure out the person who's doing all of this, but we'll have to put the trap on hold for a little while," Grayson added. "I need all the reserve deputies out looking for that SUV and dealing with the snipers."

Understandable. He had a new crime scene to process.

"Is Eric still here?" Lucas asked.

"No. He's at the DA's office getting a copy of the plea deal." Grayson paused, looked at Hailey. "If you're feeling up to it, you need to come to my office. We have Preston's recordings set up in there, and we listened to something else that you should hear."

LUCAS CERTAINLY HADN'T forgotten about the recordings that Eric had given Grayson. After all, that was one of the reasons Hailey and he had been on their way to the sheriff's office.

The other reason they had come was to set that trap that was now on hold. No way did Grayson have enough manpower to cover protecting the reserve deputy, and there'd been enough people put at risk today without adding that.

"You're sure you're steady enough to do this now?" Lucas asked her as they made their way to Grayson's office.

She nodded, didn't stop walking. He suspected Hailey was nowhere near *steady*. Not so soon after nearly being killed. But it was clear she was going to steel herself up and listen to what he hoped would give them information they could actually use. As opposed to information that would just make Hailey feel worse than she already did.

Grayson had two laptops in his office, and

Josh was listening to one with headphones. Since there were hours of recordings, there was no telling how long it would take to go through them all.

"I've loaded the recordings into audio files that we can access from several computers," Grayson explained, and he hit the play button, motioning for Hailey and Lucas to sit. "This is the first conversation that's connected to you," he added, looking at Hailey. "It was recorded about two weeks before the start of Preston's trial."

It didn't take long before Lucas heard a man's voice. Preston, no doubt. "We need to do something about your sister," he said.

"I could talk to Laura." It was Colleen who responded. Lucas recognized her voice from the phone conversation she'd had with Hailey.

"Talking won't help," Preston snapped. "She could send me away for life. Is that what you want?"

"No. Of course not." Colleen paused for several seconds. "What do you want me to do?"

Preston, however, didn't hesitate. "Find something I can use against her, something to neutralize her."

"There wasn't anything to find," Colleen insisted. "Nothing illegal, anyway."

"Then make Laura believe that I'll hurt you if

she doesn't back off. She loves you. She'll protect you. If that doesn't work, plant something that'll get her to stop."

"Plant what?" Colleen asked.

"Anything illegal. I don't care what, just something to make the cops think she's trying to cover up her own crimes by pinning them on me. You're a whiz with the computer, so hack into hers and see what you can do."

Grayson hit the pause button and turned to Hailey. "I'm guessing this is the first you're hearing of any of this?"

Hailey nodded. "I knew Colleen didn't want me to testify against Preston, but she never said anything about this false threat of making me think he would hurt her."

"Maybe because Colleen thought something like that wouldn't work with you?" Grayson pressed.

"No. It might have worked." Then Hailey groaned softly. "But I wouldn't have just stopped pursuing Preston. I would have just figured out a way to keep Colleen safe."

Lucas hoped Hailey would have done that by going to the cops. She didn't know him then. They hadn't met until after Preston's trial and after she'd entered WITSEC, but she'd obviously been working with some cops that she'd trusted.

"As far as I know," Hailey continued, "Colleen didn't plant anything illegal on my computer." She took a deep breath as if to steady her nerves. This was no doubt only adding salt to the wounds, but Lucas knew this wasn't the last of the things she probably wouldn't want to hear.

"Preston and Colleen sound *friendly*," Lucas commented. "Just how friendly were they?"

"I don't know for sure, but since Colleen didn't do what Preston wanted her to do—I mean, by planting something to frame me—then maybe they weren't as friendly as Preston seems to think they were."

Lucas latched right onto that. "You think Colleen was afraid of him?"

Another headshake from Hailey. Then a shrug. "Maybe, but Colleen never gave any indication of that."

"Of course, we haven't had a chance to listen to all the recordings," Grayson said. "But so far there's nothing about Colleen being afraid. Nothing about the specific nature of Colleen and Preston's relationship, either." He paused. "In fact, I'm betting that the recordings have been edited with parts cut out."

"You think Eric did that?" Lucas asked.

"Maybe. But it could have just as well been Colleen or Preston. The CSI lab is analyzing the originals to see if there have been any alterations. If not, it makes the second recording—well—all the more interesting. It's the last one, made the final day of Preston's trial. He was out on bond, but since he was convicted just a few hours later and put in jail, he didn't have a chance to go home again."

Grayson pressed the play button again, and like on the other recording, Lucas immediately heard Colleen's voice. "It's true. Hailey does have something incriminating on Eric. I'm not sure exactly what, but she won't use it against him. She wants to hold it over your head to make sure you don't go after her."

Preston cursed. "If I end up behind bars, you need to fix that for me. Swear that you will."

"I will," Colleen answered without hesitation.

"You'll also need to pay your sister back for what she's doing to me," Preston continued. "Understand?"

Again, Colleen didn't hesitate. "I understand."

Even though Hailey didn't make a sound, Lucas could see her body tense, and he put his hand over hers. It must have felt like a punch to the gut to hear her sister basically say that she would get revenge for Preston. Was that what the attacks were all about? Payback?

Colleen didn't say anything else because Preston's phone rang. "I need you to step out while I take this call," he told her. He didn't continue for several seconds, probably until Colleen had left. "How's my favorite FBI agent?" Preston said to the caller. There was plenty of sarcasm in his voice. "Have you tied up the loose ends for me?"

Lucas moved closer to the computer so that he wouldn't miss a word. This had to be the dirty agent.

"Please tell me that Preston gives us a name during this conversation," Lucas said to Grayson.

"Sorry, there's no mention of a name, but there's other info that might be able to help us ID him."

Good. Lucas kept listening.

"If the worst happens and I'm convicted," Preston continued, "go to my bank in San Antonio and destroy everything in the safe deposit box."

Too bad they couldn't hear how the agent responded to that, but Lucas knew what Grayson meant about that *other info*. "You're getting surveillance footage from Preston's bank?"

Grayson nodded. "It'll take a while, though, because I need a court order." Which he would get for something like this. Eric might have been telling the truth when he said the recordings could help them arrest Minton.

"One final thing," Preston said to the caller. "If Colleen doesn't take care of the situation, I want you to kill Laura."

Lucas didn't think it was his imagination that Hailey became even paler than she already was, and he did more than hold her hand this time. He slipped his arm around her. Yes, she already knew someone was trying to kill her, but it was hard to hear it spelled out like that. But Hailey eased out of his grip and reached for the phone.

"I'm calling my sister," she insisted, snatching up Grayson's desk phone and putting it on speaker.

No one stopped her, mainly because Lucas didn't expect Colleen to answer. But she did. She answered on the first ring.

"I just heard proof that Preston asked you to kill me," Hailey said without issuing a greeting. "Don't bother to deny it. What I want to know is if you're carrying through on his wishes."

"No." Colleen's voice was shaky, and she didn't jump right into an explanation. She took several moments. "I couldn't go through with it."

"You're sure about that?" Lucas snapped. "You were near the ranch today when there was another attack."

"I was lured there." Colleen paused again. A long time. "I thought I was meeting someone who could give me information. But it turned out to be a hoax."

"What kind of information?" Hailey demanded.

More hesitation. "About this nightmare that's happening. Hailey, I'm so sorry, but I'm not behind the attacks. Things haven't always been good between you and me, but I'm not a killer."

"Then who is?" Hailey pressed. "Who's the dirty agent who was working for Preston? Is it Minton?"

"Maybe." Colleen gave a heavy sigh. "I wish I could say it's him, but I'm not sure there is an agent. Not a real one, anyway. I think it could have been one of Eric's henchmen posing as an agent."

Interesting. This was the first Lucas was hearing of this possibility. "Why would you say that?"

"Some things just aren't adding up, and I think Eric duped Preston into believing he had an agent on the take. I also believe Eric might have used that fake agent to spy on his father. I'm so sorry," Colleen repeated. Lucas heard something in her voice. Guilt maybe. Maybe fear.

It wasn't fear, though, that he saw on Hailey's face. It was pure frustration. Something he felt as well. Because Colleen was stalling, and he wanted to know why.

"Why did you erase the files that Hailey had on Eric?" Lucas demanded.

"I swear, I didn't have a choice."

Lucas huffed. "That's not an answer. Why did you do it?"

Colleen hesitated again before a hoarse sob tore from her mouth. "Because it was part of the ransom demand."

Lucas looked at Hailey to see if she knew what the heck Colleen was talking about. Clearly she didn't.

"A ransom?" Hailey questioned.

Colleen sobbed again. "For my baby with Preston."

And with that, Colleen ended the call.

Chapter Eleven

A baby.

Hailey sat there for a moment, stunned with the news her sister had just dropped on them, and then she pressed Redial. Colleen didn't answer. The call went straight to voice mail.

"Colleen could be lying," Lucas pointed out.

Yes. This could all be some kind of ploy to make them believe that her sister was being manipulated into doing these things. But it was also possible.

"Preston and she could have had an affair." Hailey was talking more to herself than anyone specific, but it prompted Grayson to take out his phone.

"I'll have someone run a search of birth certificates," Grayson explained. "Any idea how old a baby would be if it exists?"

Even though the thoughts were racing in Hailey's head, she forced herself to think. "Preston went to prison eighteen months ago, so unless he had conjugal visits, the baby would have to be at least nine months old. But possibly older. Colleen never said anything about being pregnant, though."

Not exactly surprising, because Colleen and she hadn't been on the best terms when Hailey had entered WITSEC.

"If there really is a baby, then Eric could have kidnapped it to get Colleen to cooperate," Lucas suggested. "*If,*" he emphasized.

Yes, that was a big if. But even if Colleen did have a child, that didn't mean it was Preston's. She could have gotten pregnant by someone else after he went to prison.

Grayson was still on the phone, but Hailey heard a familiar voice coming from the squad room. And she groaned. It was Minton, and she didn't want to go another round with him today. Obviously, though, that's what was going to happen, because he was demanding to see Lucas and her.

"I'll handle this," Lucas said, getting to his feet.

It was tempting to let him do just that, but Hailey got up as well so she could see what had prompted this latest visit from one of their suspects. Of course, he was no longer at the top of her list because Colleen was now in that particular spot.

"I'm getting a court order for those recordings," Minton informed them the moment he caught sight of them. "My boss will be here any minute with it. You need to turn over copies of those recordings Eric gave you along with the files you have on Eric. And I want them now."

"We'll just wait for that court order if you don't mind," Lucas answered. "Even if you do mind, we'll wait."

Hailey had no idea if there really was a court order or if this was a bluff on Minton's part. But she could clear up one thing for him now. "My sister hacked into my online storage and erased the info I had on Eric."

Minton's eyes were already narrowed, and they stayed that way. "You expect me to believe that?"

She lifted her shoulder. "I don't care what you believe, but it's the truth."

Now Minton cursed. "No way would Colleen help Eric."

Not voluntarily. But Hailey had to rethink that, too. With all the possible lies being bantered about, Hailey had no idea if Colleen even despised Eric.

"Why would Colleen have done something like that?" Minton pressed.

Hailey looked at Lucas to see if he had an opinion on how much or how little she should say, and he took the lead from there.

"Colleen perhaps had a child who's been kidnapped. You know anything about that?" Lucas asked.

Hailey carefully watched Minton's reaction, and now his eyes widened in disbelief. Or perhaps he was faking that response. Because if someone had indeed taken Colleen's child, it could have been Minton. Yes, Eric had a stronger motive, but Minton could have done it to force Colleen to do whatever was necessary to make sure his crimes weren't revealed.

Anything, including those attacks to murder Hailey.

"This is the first I'm hearing of a child," Minton answered. "It's true?"

"We're trying to confirm it now," Lucas assured him.

Minton took out his phone. "I want to talk to Colleen. Where is she?"

Hailey shook her head. "Your guess is as good as mine."

It didn't surprise her that Minton had Colleen's number in his phone. After all, her sister was part of the investigation into Preston. And now Eric. It also didn't surprise her when Colleen didn't answer.

"I'll have someone from the bureau look for her," Minton said, and he fired off a text.

Finding Colleen still wasn't within the FBI's jurisdiction, but at this point Hailey just wanted her sister found so she could be brought in for questioning. She only hoped that whoever Minton had contacted wasn't as dirty as he possibly could be.

"What do you know about this so-called kidnapping?" Minton continued when he'd finished the text.

"Not much." Lucas took out his own phone. "But let me talk to someone who might know."

Hailey wasn't sure who he was going to call. When Lucas put the phone on speaker, though, the DA's office answered, and he asked to speak to Eric.

"Tell me about Colleen's baby," Lucas said the moment Eric came on the line.

"What baby?" Eric snapped.

He seemed as surprised as Minton had been. Of course, it was possible neither man had had much personal contact with her sister, so their reactions might have been genuine.

"Colleen claims someone kidnapped her baby with Preston," Lucas explained. "Was it you?"

Eric's profanity was even worse than Minton's had been earlier. "She's lying. She's doing this to get money from Preston's estate. Well, it won't work. He left everything to me in his will."

Hailey figured that was true, and maybe that was her sister's motive for this. Of course, if Colleen truly had been having an affair with Preston, then he'd probably arranged to have her receive some money before he was killed in prison. At least Hailey hoped that was the case. No way, though, would Eric want Colleen or anyone else, for that matter, to have a dime of his father's money. Eric hated Preston, but he loved the big bucks and trust fund that came with the family name.

"I want to talk to Colleen," Eric practically shouted.

"Welcome to the club," Lucas grumbled, and without even saying goodbye, he ended the call.

Minton jabbed his finger toward Lucas's phone. "That doesn't prove Eric's innocent. No way would he admit to kidnapping his half sibling. If a baby really exists, that is."

"A baby does exist," Grayson said as he came out of his office. For four little words, he got everyone's attention. He came into the squad room before he continued. "According to Texas Vital Statistics, Colleen gave birth to a daughter eleven months ago. Her name is Isabel."

The emotions flooded through Hailey. She

had a niece. Colleen had been telling the truth. About that, anyway.

"And the father?" Hailey asked.

Grayson shook his head. "No name's on the birth certificate. In Texas, Colleen would have needed written consent to include the father's name."

Maybe because it would have been too much trouble to get the consent with Preston in jail. Or perhaps Preston wasn't the father after all.

"So, where's the baby?" Minton asked, his attention volleying among Grayson, Lucas and Hailey.

None of them had an answer. Only Colleen could give them that information, and they had to find her first. But if her niece had indeed been kidnapped, Hailey wanted to help. Especially now that she was a mother herself, she couldn't stomach the thought of a baby being taken.

"I'm sorry," Lucas said to her, his voice a soothing whisper. So was the slight touch on her arm.

She looked up at him, their gazes connecting, and the look he gave her was comforting, as well. For a second or two. Then he must have remembered that it wouldn't take much for the comforting to turn to something more.

The fire.

No, it wouldn't take much at all, and now wasn't the time for that. Maybe there'd never be time. Because, like now, Lucas would continue to fight this attraction. No way did he want to go another emotional round with her, especially since she wasn't in any position to renew a relationship.

Hailey cleared her throat, hoping that would clear her head, as well. "I'll try to call Colleen again. If she doesn't answer, I can leave a voice mail so she'll know I found out I have a niece."

She turned to go back into Grayson's office to do that, but the sound of the door opening stopped her. Hailey braced herself for another visit from Eric, but it was a bulky, dark-haired man she didn't recognize. Apparently neither did Lucas, because he instantly stepped in front of her and drew his gun.

But their visitor had a gun, too. And a badge.

"You can put your weapon away," Minton insisted. "This is FBI Agent Derrick Wendell."

Judging from the now smug look on Minton's face, this was someone he wanted to see, and it didn't take Hailey long to figure out why.

"Sheriff Ryland?" Agent Wendell asked, looking at Grayson. When Grayson nodded, Wendell took a paper from his pocket. "This is a court order. You're to turn over the recordings and all evidence that's connected to Eric DeSalvo."

Grayson mumbled some profanity under his breath and took the court order to read through it. However, Hailey figured it was legit.

"The FBI has been conducting a long-time investigation into Eric and his business operations," Wendell continued. "We have reason to believe some of these operations have crossed into other states, making it a federal case."

Lucas looked at her, and even though he didn't say anything, Hailey knew what he wanted to ask her. Did she know about any of Eric's illegal interstate deals? She didn't.

But that didn't mean there weren't any.

She shook her head and was about to tell Minton and Wendell that, but Wendell's attention went to her next. "Hailey Darrow." He didn't wait for her to confirm that. "I'm here to take you into custody."

"WHAT THE HELL do you mean by that?" Lucas growled.

Even though Lucas glared at the agent, Wendell only shrugged as if the answer were obvious. It wasn't. Not to Lucas, anyway.

"Miss Darrow is a material witness in this federal investigation. Plus, someone's trying to kill her. One of Eric's henchmen, no doubt. The FBI intends to put her in custody and keep her safe so she can testify against him."

"She's already in protective custody—mine," Lucas argued. No way was he letting Hailey go with this clown. "There's proof on the recordings that Preston was dealing with a dirty agent. How do I know that agent isn't you? Or him?" he added, tipping his head to Minton.

Judging from the way Minton's face went red, he didn't appreciate that. Apparently neither did Wendell, because he scowled. But it was going to take a lot more than riled FBI agents to get Lucas to hand her over.

"I'm not dirty," Wendell insisted. "And you haven't done a good job of protecting Hailey so far."

"I'm alive." She stepped out from behind Lucas. "I'd say that's a good job, considering that someone's been trying to kill me from practically the moment I came out of a coma."

No, he hadn't done a good job. Because if he had, Lucas would have already found the person responsible for the attacks. Though he did appreciate Hailey standing up for him. But part of him didn't like it, either.

Hell. They were on the same side of this argument, and that was tearing down more barriers between them. Barriers that Lucas wanted in place until he'd worked out a whole lot of things with Hailey. Including her intentions for custody of Camden.

"Hailey can't go with you," Grayson told the agents. "I haven't even interviewed her about the attacks."

"Again, our jurisdiction," Minton argued right back.

"Possibly," Grayson said. "But the attacks might not even be related to Eric. Or the dirty agent. This could be connected to some other things that went on in Silver Creek prior to Hailey's coma."

"What things?" Wendell challenged.

"I'm not at liberty to discuss that with you right now. But it's not federal."

Grayson was sticking up for them. Sticking his neck out, too, since he could be hit with obstruction of justice if the agents could prove he was stonewalling them. Which Grayson was. But he was also buying Hailey some time. She'd already been through hell and back and definitely didn't need to be around someone who might be trying to kill her.

Minton huffed, put his hands on his hips. "Then go ahead. Interview her. Do what you need to do, but she'll be coming with us when you're done."

Grayson shook his head. "Not anytime soon." He glanced at the court order. "This applies only to the recordings, which you can have. But there's no mention of Hailey being forced to be in your *safekeeping*." There was plenty of sarcasm on that last word.

The muscles in Minton's jaw stirred, and he turned toward his fellow agent. "Get the paperwork for Hailey. I'll get the recordings."

Wendell didn't jump to leave. He glanced at all of them as if trying to figure out how to resolve this without attempting to convince a judge that it was a necessity for him to take Hailey into forced custody. But he must have realized this wasn't an argument he could win with the Ryland lawmen, because he issued a terse "I'll be back" and headed out.

"Give me the recordings now," Minton said the moment Wendell was gone. "But Hailey doesn't leave the building until Wendell gets back."

Grayson nodded, headed to his office to get them. Giving up the recordings was no big deal since Grayson had made copies of them, but Lucas needed to make sure that Wendell didn't find a judge to do Minton and Wendell's bidding. He took Hailey by the arm and led her to the break room.

Lucas called one of his fellow Rangers and asked him to keep an eye on Wendell for him, and once he'd done that, he saw to Hailey. Who was obviously even more shaken up.

"Please don't let him take me," she said, her voice with hardly any sound.

"I won't." But Lucas only hoped it didn't come to a legal showdown between them and the FBI.

He sat on the sofa next to her, and because he thought they could both use it, he made a FaceTime call to the nanny. It was something he did often while away on business so he'd be able to see his son—if not in person, then at least on the screen.

"Is everything okay?" Tillie asked the moment she answered.

"Fine," Lucas lied. Of course, Tillie must have known it was a lie, but she managed a smile.

"Camden's sleeping," she said, whispering, "but I'll carry the phone to the nursery so you can get a peek."

Hailey moved closer to him, her attention glued to the screen, and she was holding her breath. A breath she released when Camden came into view.

The baby was sleeping, all right. He was on his side, a blue blanket draped over him. Tillie moved the phone closer to his face so they could have a better look.

Hailey touched her fingers to her lips for a moment. "I wish I were there to hold him."

Yeah. So did Lucas. Being away from his son created a horrible ache in his chest. "Maybe soon," Lucas told Hailey, and he hoped that was true. He didn't want this mess with the FBI to drag on so they'd be stuck here in the sheriff's office.

Even though Camden wasn't moving and certainly nowhere near being awake, Hailey and he continued to watch him for several minutes.

Lucas thanked Tillie before he ended the call. "We'll check in again with her in a couple of hours, when Camden will be awake," he added to Hailey.

She nodded, and he figured she was trying to look a lot braver than she felt. "You're being nice to me," she said.

He wasn't sure how to respond to that, so Lucas didn't say anything. Big mistake. Because his silence caused Hailey to look up at him. Normally her looking at him wouldn't be a big deal, but they were close. Side by side. Arms touching. With their emotions running sky-high, something as simple as a look could become a trigger for this attraction.

And it was.

Lucas felt the slam of heat go through him, and before he could remind himself that kissing Hailey would be a dumber-than-dirt sort of thing to do, he lowered his head and put his mouth to hers.

He'd thought that the attraction between them couldn't get any hotter, but he had been wrong. It did, and along with the fire came the need. A need that his body remembered only a couple of seconds into the kiss. That fire and need were what had started this whole ordeal with Hailey. Apparently the ordeal was going to continue, too. Because he certainly didn't stop kissing her.

Hailey didn't stop, either. In fact, a soft sound rumbled in her throat. A sound filled with the same need and heat that Lucas was feeling. She slipped her hand around the back of his neck, pulled him closer. Not that he needed much encouragement for that, because Lucas was already moving in on her.

He deepened the kiss, took hold of her shoulder and dragged her against him. Great. Now they were body to body with the kiss raging on and on until finally he had to stop just so they could catch their breaths.

She looked at him again, silently questioning whether this was a good idea. It wasn't. But that didn't stop Lucas from going back for a second kiss. It didn't help, of course. But this time he stopped not because of air. If he didn't stop, he was going to drag her upstairs. There was an apartment up there. With a bed.

Definitely not good.

Kissing had already added too many complications to this mix, and sex would spin those complications out of control.

He was about to apologize to her, but Grayson opened the door to the break room. Hell. One look at his face and Lucas knew something was wrong.

"The FBI isn't taking Hailey," Lucas jumped to say.

Grayson shook his head. "Not yet, anyway. No, this is about Colleen."

Hailey slowly got to her feet. "What happened?"

"There's something you need to see." Grayson motioned for them to follow him, and he led them to his office.

Thankfully, Minton wasn't there. He was still across the hall in the squad room, pacing, and judging from his expression, he was riled about something other than not getting his way about taking Hailey.

"If that's something that pertains to the FBI's investigation," Minton called out, "then I want to see it."

"It's not about the investigation," Grayson assured him. "This is a family matter." Once Hailey, Lucas and he were inside the office,

Grayson locked the door, no doubt to stop the agent from barging in.

Josh was no longer in the room listening to those recordings. Or rather, the copies of the recordings. Grayson had no doubt put him in one of the interview rooms.

"What's going on?" Lucas asked, but he was almost afraid to hear the answer.

Grayson tipped his head to his desk. There was a padded envelope, opened, along with several papers. "This just arrived by courier," he explained. "There's no name on it, but I've already called the courier's office and asked them to tell me who sent it."

Lucas went closer, Hailey following right behind him, and he saw the first piece of paper. It appeared to be test results.

"DNA," Grayson supplied. "According to the person who sent it, this proves that Isabel is Colleen's baby."

"Does the test really prove it?" Hailey immediately asked.

Grayson lifted his shoulder. "This sort of thing can be faked, but it looks real. It has both the baby's DNA and a sample apparently retrieved from Colleen. Josh is calling the lab to verify." He wore a plastic glove when he moved aside the test results to show them what was beneath.

A photo.

Of a baby girl.

Hailey leaned in even closer, her gaze combing over the picture. She nodded. "The baby definitely resembles Colleen."

Of course, they'd known Colleen had a child, but Lucas figured all of this was leading to something bad.

It was.

"This was the final thing in the envelope," Grayson said, showing them another piece of paper. "It's a ransom demand—for a quarter of a million. But there's another demand. The kidnappers say if Hailey doesn't personally turn over everything she has on the DeSalvo investigation, then Colleen will never see the child again."

Chapter Twelve

Hailey heard every word of what Grayson said. Saw it, too, written in the ransom demand. But it still took a moment to sink in.

Mercy.

If this was real, then her niece could be in grave danger. It didn't matter that she'd never seen the child. Hailey still loved her and wanted to protect her.

"No," Lucas said before Hailey could speak. "You're not going to do this."

Since she was about to tell him that she would indeed do it, he'd obviously known what she was thinking. "I have the money in savings. It's from my father's life insurance. I've never spent any of it, and it's in a bank in San Antonio."

"The money's not the problem," Lucas argued.

Yes, she knew what he meant. It was the *personally* part of the demand. Someone wanted her dead, and this could be a trap to lure her out into the open.

"But we can't just let them disappear with the baby," she snapped. What she felt was pure frustration because Lucas and she were both right. She couldn't go out to deliver anything, but she also couldn't just give up on getting back the baby.

"Just sit," Grayson suggested to her. "We'll work this out somehow."

His phone buzzed, and he lifted his finger in a wait-a-second gesture. Since the caller had gotten Grayson's full attention, Hailey figured it had to be about the kidnapping.

"Eric or Minton could have taken the baby," Hailey tossed out there.

Lucas nodded. "Or this could be something Colleen concocted. We don't know what her real motives are."

True, but it sickened her to think that her sister might be using her own child to do whatever it was she was trying to do. Plain and simple, maybe this was about the money.

"Even though my mother adopted Colleen, she didn't leave Colleen any money from her life insurance," Hailey told Lucas. "She and my mother were on the outs at the time of her death, and she left it solely to me. I offered to share it with Colleen, but she was so angry at being cut out of the will that she refused."

"Was Colleen angry enough to do something like pretending to kidnap her own daughter?"

Hailey had to shrug. "Colleen was always angry about a lot of things. Still…this doesn't feel like something she'd do."

Of course, she'd been wrong about Colleen before. She hadn't thought her sister would delete those files she'd stashed away about Eric. Which was a reminder that she didn't have a key part of what the kidnappers were demanding.

"If we can work out a deal with the kidnappers so I don't personally have to deliver their demands, I'll need to put together some fake files to give them."

Lucas didn't give her his opinion on that because Grayson finished his call and turned to them. "That was the agency for the courier who delivered the package. The person paid in cash, and according to his driver's license, his name is Eldon Silverton. It's fake," Grayson quickly added.

Hailey didn't even bother to groan because it had been such a long shot, anyway. She seriously doubted that the kidnappers would have used someone who could be identified and therefore linked back to them. Or rather, linked back to the person who'd orchestrated all of this.

"What about security cameras?" Lucas asked. "Does the courier agency have them?"

Grayson shook his head. "I think we've struck out with the courier. With the lab, too, because it was Darrin Sandmire who ordered the lab results."

Darrin was the man who'd tried to kill her the night she'd been put in a coma. According to Colleen, he'd been behind the attack shortly after Hailey left the hospital.

Darrin was also dead.

So, yes, that meant they had indeed struck out since they couldn't question Darrin about it. But something about that didn't make sense.

"Why would the person behind the kidnapping use Darrin for this?" she asked. "Why not just use someone with a fake ID?"

"It was to convince us that this is real," Lucas answered, and it prompted Grayson to nod. Thankfully, Lucas continued with his explanation, because Hailey wasn't following this. "We know Darrin's a thug. *Was* a thug. The kidnappers wanted us to understand that a thug like this was involved. That way, we could be sure the baby was truly in danger."

All of that made sense, but it also tightened the knot in her stomach. Because if a snake like Darrin had been involved, there was no telling who had the baby now.

"Let me take care of Minton," Grayson said. "And then we'll try to contact Colleen again. From now on, any conversation with her needs to be recorded."

And Hailey knew why. Her sister might be involved in this crime in some way, and anything Colleen said might lead them to the truth.

When Grayson unlocked the door and threw it open, Minton was standing right there. It was possible he'd heard some or even all of what they'd said, and he clearly wasn't happy about being excluded.

"You need to leave," Grayson ordered him before Minton could get out a word. Lucas went to his cousin's side. "Until you have papers putting Hailey in FBI custody, you have no right to be here," Grayson added.

Minton had never been a happy-looking person, and Grayson's words only made it worse. "I'm an FBI agent."

"Which gives you no right to be here. This is the sheriff's office, and last I checked, I'm the sheriff. You're leaving, and that's not a request. You can come back when and only when you have something to convince me to turn over Hailey to you."

Minton still didn't budge. He threw glances at all of them, his glare lingering on Hailey for a few long moments.

"You'll regret this," Minton said, and it sounded like a threat. He turned and stormed out.

Grayson and Lucas stood in the doorway and watched the man leave, and they didn't move until Hailey heard the front door slam.

"Make sure he doesn't come back," Grayson told one of the deputies.

He returned to his desk, handed Hailey the phone and put the recorder right next to it. Hailey pressed in the number, and it rang. And rang.

Her heart dropped when it went to voice mail.

"Colleen, I need to talk to you right away," Hailey said once she was able to leave a message. "We got a ransom demand from the kidnappers of your baby. Please call me back ASAP."

She was about to put the phone away, but it rang before she could do it. Hailey answered it as soon as Grayson hit the record button again, and she immediately heard her sister's voice.

"The kidnappers got in touch with you?" Colleen asked. "How? When?" She certainly sounded like a mother who'd had her child taken.

"A package was delivered to the Silver Creek Sheriff's Office," Lucas answered. "There's a demand for a quarter of a million and any info Hailey has on the DeSalvo family. They want her to deliver everything to them herself. Now, who's behind the kidnapping?"

"I don't know. I swear, I don't. But I'll pay them whatever it takes to get back my baby. Where and when do they want Hailey to make the drop?"

Colleen made this sound as if it were a done deal, that Hailey would indeed be involved in the exchange, but Hailey figured no way would Lucas let that happen.

"We'll go over all the details with you," Lucas said. "But only if you come here to the sheriff's office. I have some questions for you."

Hailey guessed that Colleen would come up with an excuse as to why that couldn't happen. After all, she'd stonewalled them practically from the start of this nightmare. And her sister did hesitate for a couple of seconds.

"All right," Colleen answered. "I'm just up the street and can be there in a few minutes. But please come out and watch for me. Draw your gun, too. Because when I come out in the open, they'll try to kill me."

"Who's trying to kill you and why?" Lucas snapped. But he was talking to himself, because Colleen had already hung up.

Hell. It didn't make sense that someone was trying to kill Colleen. Especially not the kidnappers. They'd probably want her alive so she would push Hailey to pay the ransom.

Maybe.

And maybe the idea was to kill Hailey when she delivered the money and files. Then, also murder Colleen so that anything the sisters had learned about the DeSalvo family would die with them. Of course, that theory worked only if Colleen was innocent. The jury was out on that. Still, Lucas couldn't risk her being gunned down if she was truly out to rescue her child.

"Wait here," Lucas warned Hailey.

She took hold of his arm. "It's too risky for you to go out there." The very thing she'd said to him when he was meeting Minton at the ranch.

That hadn't turned out so well, but Hailey must have realized they didn't have much of a choice about this, because her grip melted off him. "Just be careful," she added.

There was plenty of emotion in her voice, and Lucas didn't think all that emotion was related only to what was about to happen. No. That kiss was playing into this. It had deepened things between them. Had upped the stakes. And that wasn't good, because they were both already distracted enough without adding higher stakes.

"I mean it," Lucas warned her. "Stay put."

He headed toward the front door with Grayson following right behind him. Both drew their weapons. However, they didn't actually go outside. They stayed in the doorway, Lucas looking up one side of the street and Grayson the other. One of the deputies hurried to the window. All of them preparing for what might be another attack right on Main Street.

But there was no sound of shots. No sign of Colleen, either. Not at first, anyway, but then Lucas spotted someone on the sidewalk just two buildings up from the sheriff's office. Not Colleen, though.

Eric.

Lucas didn't like the timing of the man's arrival, and apparently Eric didn't like it much, either, when he spotted Grayson's and Lucas's weapons. He cursed as he got closer.

"Are the guns really necessary?" Eric asked.

"They're not for you," Lucas assured him. "There might be gunmen in the area."

That put plenty of alarm on Eric's face. Alarm that he could have been faking, but it still got him running toward them. Lucas considered not letting him in, but if Colleen was innocent and she saw Eric out front, that might send her back into hiding.

"Frisk him," Lucas told the deputy when Eric went into the reception area.

Lucas barely spared Eric a glance. Instead he kept his attention on Main Street, and he finally saw more movement. It was in the same area where Eric had just been. But the person wasn't on the sidewalk but rather peering around the corner of a shop.

Definitely Colleen.

Lucas motioned for her to come to them. She didn't. Not right away. She kept looking around. Not just up and down the streets but also on the rooftops. Colleen definitely seemed concerned about being gunned down. Lucas was concerned about that, as well, but if she was in danger, then that alley wasn't a safe place. Heck, nowhere out in the open was safe.

Colleen finally came out and raced toward them. She was limping, maybe an injury from her car accident, and judging from her expression, she wasn't just afraid but also in pain. The moment she reached the door, Grayson pulled her inside.

"What's he doing here?" she snarled, looking at Eric.

"I could ask you the same thing," Eric countered.

"Take Eric to an interview room," Grayson told the deputy who was still in the process of frisking the man.

"I don't want to be put away in an interview room," Eric protested. "I need to talk to Colleen."

Lucas was about to tell him, "Tough." But Colleen spoke first. "Did you kidnap my baby?"

Her voice was shaking. So was she. And that was no doubt what prompted Hailey to come out of Grayson's office and go to her sister. Something Lucas definitely didn't want her to do. Especially when Eric stepped in front of her. Eric wasn't facing Hailey, though, but rather Colleen.

"You really had a baby?" he demanded.

"Yes," Colleen snapped, "and someone took her. Was it you?"

Eric stared at her as if trying to sort all of this out. Of course, maybe he already had it sorted out if he'd been the one to kidnap the child.

"No. I didn't. Is there DNA proof?" Eric pressed. "Real DNA proof that hasn't been faked by you?"

"There is proof," Grayson verified. "Now, let's all move away from the windows." He pointed to Eric. "You either leave or go in the interview room."

Eric's chin came up. "I'm not leaving until I see solid evidence that I have a half sibling."

"Arrest him," Grayson told the deputy without hesitation. "He's obstructing justice."

Eric howled out a protest, moved out of the deputy's grip. He glared at all of them before he stormed out of the sheriff's office. Good. One less pain to deal with.

"What did the kidnappers send you?" Colleen asked the moment Eric was gone.

But Lucas didn't get a chance to show her. That's because his phone rang, and he saw Unknown Caller on the screen.

Usually not a good sign.

"Record it," Grayson said, and Josh hurried to get a recorder from his desk so that Lucas could do that.

Grayson's phone rang, too, and he stepped into the hall to take it. He motioned for Lucas to go ahead and answer his call. Lucas did, and he put it on speaker.

"Are you ready to talk?" the caller immediately said.

It was a man, but Lucas didn't recognize the voice. "About what?"

"The kids, of course. You want to get them back, right?"

Every muscle in Lucas's body tightened. "Kids?"

"Yeah. Colleen's girl and your boy. We have them both."

Chapter Thirteen

The panic slammed through Hailey so fast that she couldn't speak, couldn't breathe. But she could feel, and what she was feeling was the sheer terror after learning that someone had taken her son.

Lucas didn't respond to the caller. He looked at Grayson, and Hailey could tell from his expression that something had gone wrong.

Oh, God.

"The ranch is under attack," Grayson said, confirming her fears.

"Do they really have Camden?" Lucas asked.

Grayson shook his head, then cursed. "They're sorting that out now. An SUV armed with gunmen broke through the gate. Mason and the others responded, but it's chaos there."

"Told you," the caller taunted.

"They might not have him," Lucas tried to

assure her. But he didn't look convinced of that any more than she was.

Hailey wanted to know how in the world this had happened. She wanted to scream, run outside, find the nearest vehicle and hurry to the ranch. Lucas must have known what was going through her mind, because he took hold of her arm and had her sit at the desk next to Josh. No way could she stay put, though. She got up and started pacing.

"Let's just wait for a report from Mason," Lucas told her. He motioned to Josh who was at his desk, and Lucas mouthed, "Try to trace the call."

"Yeah, and Mason will soon tell you that we have the boy," the caller added. "And now it's time to talk about how you get both kids back."

"Prove to me that you've got him first," Lucas insisted. "You sent a picture of the girl, but I don't have anything to convince me that you truly have my son."

"Soon. I'll give you proof before our little exchange happens, and if you do what you're told, I'll give you the kids."

"I swear we'll do whatever you ask," Colleen blurted out. "Just please don't hurt them."

"Nobody will get hurt if you follow my instructions to a T."

Hailey didn't put much trust in a snake who

would kidnap babies, but she moved closer to the phone so that she wouldn't miss a word of those instructions. It was so hard to focus, though, with the tornado of bad thoughts going on in her head.

"The price is now a half million," the man said. "All because there are two of them now. Go ahead and start gathering the money. I'll give you an hour—"

"That's not enough time," Lucas interrupted. He was almost certainly stalling the kidnapper to give Josh more time to trace the call. "The money has to come from a bank in San Antonio. It'll take a while for them to pull together that kind of cash."

"All right, you have until morning. And no, don't ask for more time than that, because it's all you're going to get. Along with the money, Hailey's got to give us the files she has on the DeSalvos."

Files that she didn't have. Because Colleen had deleted them. Colleen opened her mouth, maybe to tell the kidnapper just that, but Hailey shook her head, stopping her. If this man learned that the files were gone, it might compromise the ransom and rescue. Hailey would just come up with some fake files to give them.

But there was something about this particular kidnapper's request that didn't make sense.

Hailey had assumed that Colleen had deleted the files to appease the person who'd kidnapped her baby. If she'd done that, though, then this man wouldn't be demanding them now, because he would know the files no longer existed.

"Hailey won't be delivering anything to you," Lucas argued. "You'll get the money and the files, but someone else will be doing the drop."

The kidnapper paused for several heart-stopping moments. If this man insisted she deliver the goods, she'd have to do it, of course. But it would be a suicide mission. Still, she'd go through with it if it meant Camden and her niece were safe.

"All right," the kidnapper finally said. "Not Hailey."

Hailey's breath swooshed out, but she certainly didn't feel any relief. She waited for the other shoe to drop, and it didn't take long.

"You and Eric DeSalvo will bring the money and the files." The kidnapper's words hung in the air.

Grayson and Lucas exchanged a glance, but she could see Lucas's answer in his eyes before he even spoke. "Why Eric?" he asked.

"Let's just say Eric will be bringing some cash of his own. For those files."

So Eric was being blackmailed. Or at least, according to this man he was.

Lucas huffed. "I'll have to work it out with Eric—"

"Just do it," the kidnapper snapped. "I'll call you back with the drop-off point. Have everything ready to go."

"I got the kidnapper's location from the cell tower," Josh said the moment the man ended the call. "It's coming from Sweetwater Springs. I'll get the sheriff to send someone out there."

Hailey latched onto that like a lifeline. Maybe the sheriff could find them and put an end to this.

While Josh contacted the Sweetwater Springs sheriff, Hailey went to Grayson to see if he'd heard anything about what was happening at the ranch. He had the phone pressed to his ear, and while she could hear someone talking on the other end of the line, she couldn't make out what the person was saying.

Lucas came closer to her, and he slipped his arm around her waist. Waiting. And no doubt praying, as Hailey was doing.

"I'll wait to talk to Eric," Lucas explained.

Yes, but it would have to be done. Well, it would unless they managed to end this kidnapping. But Eric would still have to be brought in to answer questions about whether or not he was being blackmailed about those blasted files.

"I didn't know you two were back together," Colleen said.

Hailey glanced at her sister, ready to explain that it wasn't like that between Lucas and her, but she didn't want to waste the energy. Besides, it seemed a strange observation to make when their children could be in grave danger.

Grayson pressed the end call button, his attention going straight to Lucas and Hailey. "Mason and the ranch hands are closing in on the trespassers. There are three of them. And we still don't know if they took Camden. It shouldn't be long, though, before Mason calls back."

A second was too long, and Hailey's legs suddenly felt ready to give way.

Josh finished his call and joined them just outside Grayson's office. "I know the timing for this is bad, but I found out something about that surveillance footage from the bank."

Hailey certainly hadn't forgotten about that. It was the security feed that was supposed to show the dirty agent Preston had sent to destroy whatever was in his safe deposit box.

"It was Eric," Josh said.

It took Hailey a moment to get what he was

saying. "Eric?" she asked. "Why would he be on that footage?"

Josh shrugged. "He'll have to answer that. Have to answer, too, what was in the box, since there's no security footage for that."

Hailey tuned out the rest of what Josh was saying when Grayson's phone rang. The sound shot through the room, shot through her, too, and Grayson answered it as fast as he could. What he didn't do was put the call on speaker. Probably because he wanted to buffer any bad news that he got. But that wasn't a bad news kind of look on his face. He blew out a quick breath.

"Camden's safe," Grayson relayed.

Suddenly she was in Lucas's arms. This time, though, not because of a kiss but because they were both overcome with relief. Relief that Colleen wasn't sharing. She went back into the squad room and sank down into one of the chairs. Hailey hoped she was having that reaction simply because she was still terrified for her daughter and not because her sister had planned this failed kidnapping.

"Is everyone okay?" Lucas asked Grayson.

"Yes. The attackers didn't get into your house. Tillie's shaken up, of course, but she said Camden's too little to know what was going on. She hid with him in the bathroom."

Good. That was probably the safest place for her to have been, but it ripped at Hailey's heart to know that her precious son, the nanny and everyone at the ranch had been put in that kind of danger.

"One of the attackers is dead," Grayson went on. "The other two escaped, but Mason called in help to look for them."

She figured the men were long gone by now, but if they could get an ID on the dead one, it might lead them back to who'd hired him.

"I need to see Camden," Hailey insisted.

Lucas didn't even argue with that. He looked at Grayson. "Can you spare a deputy to go with us?"

"Josh can do it." Grayson didn't get to add more because Lucas's phone rang.

Unknown Caller was on the screen again. Lucas waited until Grayson turned on the recorder before he answered it.

"So, we didn't get your boy," the kidnapper said. It was the same man who'd called earlier. "Not this time, anyway. But there's always tomorrow."

The muscles tightened in Lucas's jaw, and Hailey could tell he wanted to go through the phone lines and rip this guy to pieces. Hailey did, too. But more than anything, she just wanted to hold her baby and make sure he truly was safe.

"You'll still pay the ransom if you want your sister's kid back," the kidnapper insisted. "Get that money together. Those files, too, and I'll be in touch." And he ended the call.

"I'll have the call analyzed," Grayson volunteered. "To see if he's still in Sweetwater Springs. The three of you go ahead and leave."

"But what about my daughter?" Colleen asked, getting to her feet. "You can't just leave while that monster has her."

"Staying here won't help her," Lucas answered. He hooked his arm around Hailey, and along with Josh, they started toward the door. "When the kidnapper calls with drop-off instructions, I'll come back."

Hailey hoped not. Maybe they could work out a different deal. One that didn't include Lucas, her or anyone in his family. Perhaps Eric could do this solo.

There was a cruiser parked out front, and the three of them hurried to get in it. Josh took the wheel. She thought Lucas would ride in the front, but he got in the backseat with her. He brushed a quick kiss on her forehead. A kiss no doubt of relief, and he kept watch around them. So did Josh.

There was a storm moving in, and the sky

was already getting dark, but Hailey hoped the rain would hold off until they made it to the ranch. She didn't want anything to slow them down.

Josh certainly wasn't moving slowly. He was speeding through town, and like Lucas, he was also keeping watch.

"You think Colleen could have been the one to arrange this attack?" Lucas asked. It was a question that hadn't been far from her mind.

"It's possible. But even if she wasn't the mastermind, she could have known about it. Getting Camden could have been part of the kidnappers' demands to her."

Of course, Colleen hadn't said a thing about a demand like that, but it still could have happened. If Colleen was truly desperate to get her daughter back, then she might be willing to do anything. That could include having Camden taken.

Because if the kidnappers had him, they had the ultimate bargaining tool to get Lucas and her to cooperate.

Josh had just made it out of town when Lucas's phone rang again. Hailey hoped it wasn't the kidnapper calling to give them an immediate drop for the ransom. But it was Grayson. Hailey felt a new slam of fear and prayed that nothing else had gone wrong at the ranch.

"Pull over and check the cruiser," Grayson said the moment Lucas answered the call.

"What's wrong?" Josh and Lucas asked in unison.

"It might be nothing, but a waitress from the diner across the street said about thirty minutes ago she saw somebody walking by the cruiser. A man she didn't recognize. She said at one point the guy appeared to drop something, and he stooped down out of sight for a couple of seconds."

"Hell." Lucas added some more profanity as Josh pulled to the shoulder of the road. "Why didn't she tell you this sooner?"

"She got busy with some customers and just now got a break. Like I said, it might be nothing. I just want to be sure."

Judging from Lucas's and Josh's reactions, though, it could be some kind of tracking device. Or worse.

"I didn't see anyone around the cruiser," Hailey said.

But then, they'd had plenty of distractions with Minton, Eric and Colleen all there. Plus there'd been the calls from the ranch about the attack and those from the kidnapper.

"Stay inside the cruiser until I check it out," Lucas told Josh and her.

She hated that he was going out there again,

but Grayson was right. They had to be certain no one had tampered with the vehicle.

Lucas already had his gun drawn, and he stepped out. Josh opened his door, too, no doubt in case this became an ambush. But there really was no place for attackers to hide on this particular stretch of the road. There were no trees, just flat pasture, and the ditches weren't particularly deep. She also couldn't see any vehicles either ahead of or behind them.

Hailey held her breath, waiting as Lucas went around the cruiser. He was moving quickly. Until he got to the rear of the vehicle. Because she was watching him so closely, she saw the instant alarm on his face.

"Get out now!" Lucas shouted. "There's a bomb."

Lucas felt his heart slam against his chest.

He didn't take the time to kick himself for not checking out the cruiser before hurrying Hailey into it. He should have gone over every inch of it before they left the sheriff's office. But they'd been so eager to get to the ranch and check on Camden, so he hadn't done it.

Now it might cost them their lives.

Josh was out of the vehicle within seconds, mainly because his door was already open, but Hailey was struggling with hers. Lucas threw it open for her, dragging her out, and he started running with her in tow. But they weren't moving nearly fast enough. They had to put some distance between them and the car, so he scooped her into his arms and raced toward the pasture.

They made it only a few yards past the ditch, though.

The blast ripped through the air, throwing them forward and onto the ground. Lucas scrambled to cover Hailey's body with his and hoped that the flying debris didn't kill them.

Chunks of the cruiser came crashing down. Most of the pieces were in flames, and the other jagged shards fell into the pasture all around them.

"Josh?" she said, no doubt checking to make sure he'd gotten out.

He had. Lucas's cousin was on the ground only about two yards away, and from what he could see of him, he didn't have any injuries. In fact, he was already calling for backup.

"Josh is okay," Lucas assured her.

But Hailey was a different matter. When she looked up at him, he saw the two small cuts on her forehead. Probably from the fall. Maybe she hadn't broken any bones or suffered any internal injuries.

He glanced back at the cruiser. What was

left of it, anyway. It was now a fireball, and if they'd been inside when that bomb had gone off, they'd all be dead.

"We need to get into the ditch," Lucas told them.

The sound of the blast was still causing his ears to ring, and it was hard to think. However, he didn't need to think hard to know they shouldn't stay out in the open like this. Someone could be coming to finish them off.

He helped Hailey to her feet, and despite the ringing noise, he still heard the grunt of pain she made. She'd need to be checked out by a doctor. First, though, they needed to get out of here.

"Grayson's on the way," Josh relayed.

Good. They were so close to town that it wouldn't take him long to get there, but trouble could arrive ahead of him. Lucas figured whoever had planted that bomb was probably nearby so they could finish them off.

And he was right.

Within seconds after having that thought, he saw the SUV coming up the road from the direction of the town, and Lucas knew they didn't have much time. They had to take cover now. He ran toward the ditch, dropping down into it. It was shallow, too shallow, but it was the only thing they had right now.

"Stay down as far as you can get," he warned

Hailey, and both Josh and he got into crouching positions so they could return fire if necessary.

The SUV screeched to a stop just about twenty feet from them. It was hard to see just how many were inside, though, because of the black smoke coming from the cruiser. The gas tank was already gone, so there probably wouldn't be a secondary explosion, but Lucas wanted Hailey to stay down just in case. That's why he cursed when he felt her put her hand in the waist of his jeans and take his backup weapon from his slide holster.

"You might need an extra hand," she insisted.

He didn't have time to argue with her. Didn't want to turn his attention from that SUV for even a second, but he hoped like the devil that she didn't do anything to get herself hurt worse than she already was.

"Can you see how many of them there are?" Lucas asked Josh.

His cousin shook his head and then scurried down the ditch, no doubt to get a better angle. While Josh was still in motion, though, the front passenger door of the SUV flew open. The barrel of a gun appeared.

And the shot came.

Like the explosion, it ripped through the air, and the bullet slammed into the asphalt just a few inches from Lucas and Hailey. He shoved

Hailey back down, took aim and returned fire. His shot smacked against the door and sent the gunman ducking back inside the SUV.

But not for long.

The driver lowered his window and started shooting. Not just one shot, either. These came at them. A barrage of bullets that tore right through the mud and dirt in the ditch. Soon it would tear into them, too, if Lucas didn't do something.

He couldn't lift his head for long. Too risky. And if these thugs managed to kill him, then Hailey would be left as easy prey. So Lucas glanced up just long enough to get his aim. Then he lowered his head.

And he fired.

Lucas could tell from the pinging sound of the shots that he was hitting the SUV. Ideally he was hitting the gunmen, as well, but if so, that didn't stop them from continuing to fire.

"Grayson," Hailey said.

It took Lucas a moment to pick through all the noise from the gunshots to hear a welcome sound. A siren. Grayson certainly wasn't making a quiet approach, and Lucas was thankful for it. Thankful because the gunmen stopped firing.

But that wasn't the only thing they did.

Almost immediately, the driver threw the

SUV into Reverse and hit the accelerator hard. He sped backward until he reached the dirt path at the edge of the pasture and then spun the SUV around so that it was heading in the opposite direction.

Lucas came out of the ditch and started firing, hoping to shoot out the tires. Just up from him, Josh did the same. But they were too late.

The gunmen were getting away.

Chapter Fourteen

Hailey held Camden close while he slept in her arms. She wasn't sure she would ever want to let go of him again. Lucas and she had come so close to losing him.

So close to making him an orphan, too.

But Hailey didn't want to think about that. She only wanted this time with her son. Of course, Lucas wanted time with him, as well, but he was on the phone, pacing and trying to get more information from Grayson about the attack. Especially more information about who'd been in that SUV.

Since they'd gotten back to his place, Lucas had learned that the camera at the bank on Main Street had captured some footage of the SUV used in the attack. The footage wasn't clear, but the CSI lab might be able to enhance it enough so they could see the license plate number or even their attackers' faces.

Outside, the storm was finally moving in, and the rain was starting to spatter against the windows. The air felt heavy and thick, almost as if it were bearing down on them. It didn't help that the house was nearly dark, too. Lucas had turned off all the lights when they'd gotten in. Probably so anyone watching them wouldn't be able to see their shadows and know where to aim.

Lucas finished his latest call and went to her, sinking down on the sofa next to her. He didn't say anything. He just looked at her. Or rather, he looked at the cuts on her face. Tillie had tended them after Hailey had showered and changed her clothes, but they were no doubt a clear reminder of what'd happened to them.

"I'm sorry this happened," Lucas finally said.

Hailey shook her head. "It's not your fault. Remember, we're in danger because of me."

Admitting it put a lump in her throat. Brought tears to her eyes, too. She blinked them back because it wouldn't do either of them any good for her to break down and cry. Still, she lost the battle fighting it, and tears spilled down her cheeks.

Lucas cursed under his breath, pulled her to him and kissed her forehead. She was almost positive he didn't want her in his arms. Or so she thought. Until their gazes connected again.

Yes, he did want it. Even though he knew it was only breaking down more of those barriers between them.

"What about Colleen's baby?" she asked. "Have the kidnappers called back yet with the drop-off point?"

"No, but I suspect we won't hear from them until morning. I hope it's not sooner, because Grayson still hasn't convinced Eric to do the drop with me."

Hailey hoped the kidnappers changed their minds about that. She didn't want Lucas out there where he could be gunned down, and she especially didn't want him out there with Eric. If Eric was the person behind everything, then he could lead Lucas right into a trap and then use Lucas to draw her out.

And it would work.

No way would Hailey hide herself away and let Lucas be hurt or killed just to protect her.

"Grayson said there's no sign of the gunmen," Lucas continued after he looked away from her and stared at Camden. He touched his fingers to the baby's toes peeking out from the blanket.

She hadn't expected there would be, and Hailey already knew it would take the crime lab a while to get to the camera footage from the cruiser, especially since they had so many other things to process from this investigation. Which was a reminder about Eric showing up on the security footage from the bank.

"Has Grayson had a chance to talk to Eric yet?" she asked. It'd been a couple of hours since the attack. Maybe more than a couple since she hadn't been keeping up with the time. But she figured Grayson would make that a priority.

Lucas nodded. "Eric claims the only reason he went to the bank was that he listened to the recordings and wanted to get to the safe deposit box before one of his father's lackeys did."

It could be true. Could. But this was Eric, so there was no telling. "What was in the box?"

"According to Eric, nothing much. Just some records of illegal land deals and such that Preston had done over the years. He says he destroyed them since those were his father's last wishes."

Since Eric hated his father, she seriously doubted he would care a flying fig about carrying out Preston's wishes. "There must have been something in the box to incriminate Eric."

Lucas made a sound of agreement. There was no way to prove that, though. Maybe Grayson could go after Eric for destroying possible evidence, but with everything else he and his deputies had on their plates, that probably wouldn't happen soon, either.

"Minton came by the sheriff's office again,"

Lucas continued. "Of course, he says this latest attack is yet another reason for you to be in his protective custody." He paused. "If that's what you want—"

"No." And Hailey didn't even have to think about it. "I want to be here with Camden and you."

Lucas stayed quiet a moment, just long enough for her to know something was wrong. It was also plenty long enough for the feeling of panic to start spreading through her.

"Please tell me I don't have to go with Minton," she said.

"No. Well, not unless he manages to get a court order, which hasn't happened. Even then, I think we could fight it."

Good. But something else was obviously wrong, because his forehead bunched up. "Grayson and I talked about Camden, and we don't think it's a good idea for him to be here. Those attackers could try to come after him again. The ranch is secure, but he'd be better off at the main house."

The place where Mason and his family now lived. It was in the center of the ranch, which would make it harder for kidnappers to get to Camden. Still, there was a problem.

"If the kidnappers have us under surveillance, they might see that we're taking him there," Hailey pointed out.

Lucas nodded. Hesitated again. "The kidnappers want Camden only to use him to get to you."

Because Hailey was fighting the spent adrenaline and the new wave of panic, it took her a moment to figure out what he was saying. "You don't want me to be with Camden."

Another nod.

Oh, mercy. That felt like a punch to the stomach, and it caused a fresh round of tears to fill her eyes. It broke her heart to think of not having Camden close to her.

But Lucas was right.

Her baby was much safer without her around. Plus, Lucas's house was close to the main road. Too close. It would be the first place that gunmen reached if they stormed the ranch.

"How soon would Camden have to leave?" she asked.

"Soon," Lucas said. "Now would be better. I already talked to Tillie about it when you were in the shower, so she's ready. Sawyer and two ranch hands are outside patrolling, but they'll drive Tillie and Camden to the house."

That punch felt even harder, and she saw Tillie peer out from the kitchen, where she was almost certainly waiting for Lucas to break the news. The nanny gave her a sympathetic look, but Tillie was probably ready to put some distance between her and Hailey. After all, Tillie was in danger, too, simply by being around her.

"I'll take good care of him," Tillie assured her.

Hailey knew she would, but it was still hard to let go of the baby. She gave him a kiss on the cheek. Added several more. And she handed him to Lucas so he could take him to Tillie. Once he'd done that, he sent a text. No doubt to Sawyer or one of the hands, because it wasn't long before Hailey heard the sound of a vehicle pulling directly in front of the house.

"We'll come up in the morning to see him," Lucas told the nanny.

When visibility would be better, and it would be easier to spot any attackers who were trying to get close to the ranch. Of course, the visibility wasn't that good right now, which only made her fears skyrocket.

"What if they start shooting when Tillie and Camden go outside?" Hailey asked.

"There's nothing to be gained from them hurting Camden," Lucas assured her. "They want to take him, but they can't do that if he's at the main house."

It felt like a horrible loss to have these next hours taken away. But maybe Lucas and she could use that time to figure out a way to put an end to the danger. They could still set the trap using the reserve deputy to try to lure out the culprit with the promise of getting those files that Colleen had deleted.

"Stand back," Lucas told her. "I don't want you by the door when it's opened."

Yes, because it might prompt the gunmen to fire shots at her. That would put everyone, including the baby, in harm's way.

Hailey tried to hold it together but failed miserably when Lucas disarmed the security system so he could get Tillie and Camden out of the house. They didn't spend but just a couple of seconds out in the open before Sawyer got them in a cruiser. He took off with them as soon as they were inside.

Two other ranch hands stayed behind, no doubt to keep guard. Lucas did his part in keeping them safe, as well. He locked the door and reset the security system.

As fast as she could, Hailey went to the windows on the same side of the house as the road and opened the curtains. She watched as Sawyer sped out of sight.

"That's not a safe place to stand," Lucas said. He not only moved her back but also closed the curtains again. Shut off the lights, too. "You should try to get some rest," he added. "I'll call Grayson and see if there are any updates."

Hailey had every intention of moving toward the guest room where she'd been staying, but her feet suddenly seemed anchored to the floor. Her eyes seemed out of her control, too, because she started to cry again. She hated the tears. They wouldn't help anything, and in fact, they clearly made Lucas uncomfortable, because his forehead bunched up.

Lucas gave a heavy sigh and went to her. He pulled her into his arms. "It's just temporary," he reminded her.

She got the feeling he was talking about more than just Camden. He probably meant her being here in his house.

In his arms.

They stood there in the darkness with only the sound of the rain and their breaths. She could feel his heartbeat since his chest was against hers. At the moment Hailey could feel everything about him. Feel everything about herself, too.

Especially the heat.

It came, of course. It always came when she was anywhere near Lucas. It was especially there now because they were coming down from the nightmare of the attack and having to be separated from Camden.

"I'm okay," she told him, giving him an out so he could back away.

But Lucas didn't budge. "I always swore that I'd never go another round with you."

That stung, but it was exactly what she expected him to say. "Understandable. I made mistakes with you. Not the sex," Hailey quickly added. "That wasn't a mistake because we got Camden. But I messed up pretty much everything else."

A sound that could have meant anything rumbled in his chest. "I still don't think it's a good idea for us to get involved. Not like this." He glanced at the close contact between them.

Because she thought they could use some levity, she smiled. "Are you trying to convince yourself?"

"Yeah," he admitted.

The levity vanished. So did what was left of her smile. Now, that was not what she'd expected him to say. Lucas was the sort of man who kept his feelings, and his pain, close to the vest. She'd hurt him by not trusting him, and it would take him a long time to get over that.

Or maybe not.

"I'm not doing a good job of convincing myself," he added. "In fact, I'm sinking fast here. I'm trying to come up with a damn good reason why I shouldn't just strip you naked and take you to my bed."

That robbed her of what little breath she had. And it fired up every inch of her.

"I hope you can't think of a reason," she whispered.

There. She'd given him the green light that he probably didn't want. Probably wouldn't take, either.

But she was wrong.

He lowered his head, kissed her. Not a gentle I'm-still-thinking-about-this kind of kiss. It was the real deal. Long and deep. It didn't do anything to cool down her body. Just the opposite.

The kiss went on for so long that Hailey staggered a little because she couldn't breathe. Lucas caught her, tightening his grip around her, and he pulled back so they could take in some air.

He also cursed himself. And he looked down at her. Despite the darkness, she could still see a storm of a different kind brewing in his eyes. Fire mixed with the bitterness of the past.

The fire won out.

Because Lucas scooped her up in his arms, kissed her again and headed in the direction of his bedroom. He stopped along the way to kiss her again. Maybe to make one last-ditch effort at rethinking this, but they were obviously past the point of no return.

Later there'd be consequences.

But Hailey didn't want to think about those now.

She wanted only to feel, wanted to let Lucas take her to the only place she wanted to go. A place with no tears, no gunmen. It was just the two of them, giving in to the heat that had been blazing since they'd first met.

He carried her to the bed, eased her onto the mattress. He was being too gentle with her. Probably because she didn't have her full strength, but she didn't want gentle. Not with this ache starting to throb inside her.

Hailey caught onto him, dragging him closer, and ideally letting him know that she wasn't fragile. Also letting him know that there was already a need to finish what they'd started. In case he didn't get the message, she put her hand over the front of his jeans.

Yes, he got the message, all right.

He lowered the kisses to her neck. Foreplay. Definitely not overrated when it came to Lucas, though there really was no need to fan these flames any higher.

She was wearing a loaner dress that had been in a stash that some of the Ryland wives had sent over. It was loose, so Lucas had no trouble pushing it up, and she felt his hand on her bare skin. His mouth, too, when he took those kisses to her breasts. Then her stomach. He lingered there a moment before he stripped off her bra and panties.

And he kept kissing her.

Hailey didn't want to be the only one naked, though, so she went after his shirt. Not an easy task, though, since Lucas was still wearing a holster. He had to put the kisses on hold to help her with that, and the battle started up again. Hailey wanted his clothes off *now*, but Lucas was back to the kisses.

Which kept going lower.

If they continued in that direction, he was going to make her climax. Something she desperately wanted. But not like this. She wanted him inside her.

Hailey caught onto him, pulling him back up. The movement created an incredible sensation with his body sliding over hers. That made her reach for his zipper. She fumbled around and cursed, causing Lucas to smile. As he'd done with the shirt, he helped her get off the rest of his clothes.

But then he stopped. And moved away from her.

She could have sworn her heart stopped, too, but then she realized he was only getting a condom from the nightstand drawer. It brought back the memories of the other time they'd been together.

The memories got a whole lot better, though.

Lucas came back to her, and once he had on the condom, he gathered her into his arms again. Kissed her. And entered her slowly, easing into the heat of her body. Hailey hadn't thought she'd wanted gentle and easy, but this was working just fine for her. He took his time, building the fire even hotter.

It didn't last.

Couldn't.

The need soon took over, and slow and easy was done. Now it was all about finishing this. And he did. Lucas moved in her, the pace as frantic and deep as the need. Until both of them went flying right over the edge.

Chapter Fifteen

Lucas tried to get some sleep. Hard to do, though, with a naked Hailey right next to him. Especially hard to do with the thoughts racing through his head. Thoughts of tomorrow's ransom drop and of the danger to his son.

Thoughts, too, of what'd happened between Hailey and him.

He figured he should regret the sex. And in some ways he did. It was a distraction that he didn't need at a time when he should have been focused on the investigation. Still, it was hard to regret something that'd been damn good.

At least she was sleeping now. That was good. But he figured her body hadn't given her much of a choice about that. Hailey had been running on adrenaline since coming out of the coma, and she needed to rest. Because tomorrow would be a hellish day for her, as well.

Lucas only hoped he could get back Colleen's

baby without anyone getting hurt or killed. While he was hoping, he added that Eric would cooperate and do the drop with him. So far, he hadn't agreed, which meant Lucas would have to convince him or else renegotiate with the kidnappers.

Maybe Colleen wouldn't do something stupid before then.

Shortly after Hailey had fallen asleep, Lucas had gotten a text from Grayson telling him that Colleen had refused to stay at the sheriff's office any longer. Grayson hadn't had any grounds to hold her, and even though he'd reminded her that the kidnappers could be watching the place, Colleen had left anyway. At best, she was just going somewhere else to wait for the ransom drop. At worst, she was in grave danger. And Grayson didn't have the manpower to send someone out to make sure she didn't get herself into trouble.

Right now, the Rylands had enough trouble on their hands.

Lucas glanced at the laptop that he'd brought into the bedroom after Hailey had fallen asleep. It was on the nightstand next to him, and it showed the feed from the security cameras positioned all around the ranch. No doubt several of his cousins were watching the cameras, too, as was the head ranch hand. All of them looking to make sure someone didn't try to sneak onto the grounds.

So far, so good.

It was a bad night, though, for any kind of sneaking around outside. The rain was steady and heavy, and there was the occasional jag of lightning in the sky. Maybe the storm would be enough to keep the thugs from another attempt to take Camden or Hailey.

With a few strokes on the laptop keyboard, Lucas pulled up the feed from another camera. This one was in the nursery at the main house. Tillie had set up the camera so that they could see Camden. And there he was, sleeping in a crib. He was sharing the room with Mason's son, Max. Tillie was in the guest room just up the hall and would no doubt have a baby monitor next to her bed so she'd be able to hear the babies if they woke up.

As if she'd sensed what Lucas was doing, Hailey stirred, her eyes opening and her attention going straight to the screen. She smiled. Sat up.

"It's not the same as having him here with us, but it's still nice to see him," she said.

Yeah. It was. But the *us* gave Lucas some hesitation. She'd said it so easily, as if it were normal. It wasn't. And Hailey must have realized her slip, because she muttered an apology under her breath.

Lucas hated that she felt the need to apologize. Hated even more that he felt as if he should have one. Because despite the fact that she was in his bed, they were a long way from getting to the *us* stage.

Once he'd taken care of the danger, they could start working on that. And Lucas refused to believe he couldn't put an end to the attacks, because if he couldn't, it would mean Hailey and Camden going to a safe house. Or her even returning to WITSEC, but this time she would have to take Camden with her since as long as he was out there, the snake behind this could use the baby to get to Hailey.

"Colleen left the sheriff's office," Lucas told her. "Grayson couldn't talk her out of it."

Hailey gave a heavy sigh. "No, he wouldn't have been able to do that. Did Colleen say where she was going?"

Lucas shook his head. "But unless she manages to get her hands on the money, she can't do the ransom exchange." And he hoped she didn't even attempt it.

She looked at Camden again. Then Lucas. "You're no doubt thinking we messed things up big-time," she said. "And yes, I'm talking about the sex."

He let that hang in the air for a couple of seconds. Then lifted his shoulder. "Well, yeah, when I mess up, I aim for big."

She laughed, but it wasn't exactly from humor. More nerves. Something he understood. Reality was quickly settling in, and there was no way they could go back to where they'd been just hours earlier. There was no such thing as casual sex when it came to Hailey.

The silence settled between them. And it wasn't exactly comfortable. Hailey fixed her attention to the laptop and on Camden. As much as he wanted to continue looking at their son, though, he had to switch the camera back so he could help watch the security feed. That didn't do much to ease the discomfort between them.

"Just how bad do you think it'll get tomorrow?" she asked.

He considered lying and saying "not bad at all," but he couldn't make that kind of guarantee. He looked at her, though. Saw the worry on her face again, so Lucas decided to go with a half guarantee.

"I'll make it work," he assured her and brushed a kiss on her cheek.

Of course, that sparked the attraction again, along with sparking another kiss. This time not on the cheek but her mouth. Hailey moved right into the kiss, too, sliding closer and touching him.

Not good since they were naked.

That didn't stop him, though, from deepening the kiss and hauling her right against him. However, then something stopped Lucas.

It was just a soft beep, barely audible because he had the sound turned down on the laptop, but it was a sound that went through him like the lightning bolt that slashed outside.

Because it meant something or someone had triggered one of the dozens of sensors positioned all around the ranch.

The laptop was showing six different cameras, the ones positioned on the most vulnerable points of the ranch. The fence lines and the road. He looked at each of them but didn't see anything.

"Does that sound mean what I think it means?" Hailey asked. She moved away from him, her attention back on the screen.

"It could be nothing," Lucas tried to assure her. "Sometimes animals trigger the sensors. The storm could, too, if the wind knocked down a tree branch or something."

Lucas held on to that hope, but it was hard not to think the worst. Hard to stave off the knot that was already tightening in his gut. A knot that got even tighter when his phone buzzed, and he saw Mason's name on the screen.

"Any idea why the alarm went off?" Lucas immediately asked him.

"No. I'm looking through the camera feeds now, all of them, and I don't see anything. You?"

"Nothing." Lucas put the phone on speaker so he could get dressed, but he also tapped the keyboard to scroll through some of the other security feeds. "But I'll keep watching."

"Yeah, be ready just in case," Mason said, ending the call.

That sent Hailey scrambling from the bed. There were no signs of the heat and attraction on her face now. Just the fear as she grabbed her clothes and started putting them on. Fear that Lucas needed to rein in right now, because this could be a long wait to find out if anything was truly wrong.

"No one can get near the main house," he reminded her. "Not without going through a dozen ranch hands and plenty of other houses."

Since those places all had lawmen inside them, Lucas was pretty sure Camden was safe. But "pretty sure" didn't ease the knot in his stomach. He wanted a hundred percent guarantee when it came to his son, and it didn't matter where Camden was. He wouldn't have that guarantee until the person responsible for the attacks was dead or behind bars.

Hailey finished dressing—obviously she was preparing herself in case they had to go outside, but Lucas was hoping that didn't happen.

Lucas put back on both his weapons, and even though it was hard to force himself to sit down, he did for Hailey's sake. So that she'd sit, too. She did, right beside him, and they both watched the screen as he scrolled through all the feeds.

She shook her head. "I still don't see anything."

Neither did he, but it was dark, and even with the security lights, there were still plenty of shadows. Plenty of places for someone to hide, too, what with all the fences, trees and outbuildings. But if someone was out there and that person moved, then the sensors would pick him up, and the alarm would ding again.

The seconds crawled by, turning into minutes, and just when Lucas was ready to try to level his breathing, he saw something. Movement not near the fence line but near the road. It was just a blur of motion, barely in camera range and not actually on ranch land.

"What?" Hailey asked. She'd obviously noticed that he'd tensed.

"Maybe nothing," he repeated.

Lucas clicked on that specific screen, enlarged it and zoomed in on the area where he'd seen the motion. He was hoping it was a deer or an illusion caused by the rain.

But it wasn't.

It was a man dressed all in black. And he had a rifle aimed right at Lucas's house.

HAILEY COULDN'T STOP herself from gasping when she saw the man. He was lurking behind one of the trees directly across the road from the ranch.

"Oh, God," she said, and she scrambled to get the gun from Lucas's nightstand.

He took hold of her hand and had her sit next to him again. He also adjusted the view of the camera so that she could see the truck that was parked at the end of the road. Unlike the man with the rifle, the truck was actually on the ranch.

"Two of the hands are in the truck," Lucas explained, and he took out his phone and fired off a text. No doubt to warn them that there was definitely a problem.

Lucas went back to the camera angle so they could see the man, and Hailey realized he wasn't alone. There was another armed guy directly behind him.

The skin crawled on the back of her neck. Because she knew what those men wanted.

They wanted her.

And they'd try to use Camden to get her.

"Get down on the floor," Lucas instructed.

She did as he said, and he grabbed the laptop to bring it to the floor with him. The difference was he had her lie all the way down while he stayed in a sitting position. Probably so he'd be better able to respond if things turned bad in a hurry.

Hailey tried not to panic. Hard to do, though, when all she could feel was the panic and fear. Both went up a significant notch when she saw the headlights of an approaching car on the screen. The vehicle no doubt carried more thugs arriving to launch a full-scale attack.

Both the hands in the truck opened their doors, and they put out their rifles. Ready to return fire.

She gasped again when the dinging sound shot through the room. But it wasn't a security alarm. It was Lucas's phone to let him know he had a text. She saw Mason's name on the screen.

"Mason's on the line with the hands at the road," Lucas said when he read the text. "He's sending them backup right away." He cursed. "But I need to stay here."

She knew the profanity wasn't for her but the

situation. He wanted to be down there helping the hands, but all of this could be designed to have him do just that. So that she'd be alone and an easy prey.

The car came to a stop directly in front of where the hands were parked. Hailey saw another vehicle, too. A cruiser barreling down the ranch road toward the hands, the two armed men and the newly arrived vehicle. A moment later, another cruiser followed the first. So there were plenty of lawmen responding to what was no doubt about to become the scene of another attack.

"What the hell?" Lucas said, moving closer to the laptop screen.

Hailey watched as the driver of the car got out. Colleen. And her sister lifted her hands into the air as if surrendering. Colleen said something to the ranch hands, but since there was no audio, Hailey had no idea what.

But this couldn't be good.

Either her sister was part of the oncoming attack, or else she was going to be right in the middle of it.

Even though it was pouring rain, Colleen stayed outside the car, and after a very short conversation with the hands, she took out her phone. A moment later, Lucas's own phone rang. He answered it and put it on speaker.

"Hailey?" Colleen asked. Her voice was frantic. As was her expression. "You have to tell these men to let me onto the ranch."

Hailey debated how to answer that. But Lucas had no such debate with himself. "Did you bring those gunmen with you?" he asked.

"What gunmen?" Colleen's gaze began to slash all around her.

"The ones across the road."

A sob tore from Colleen's mouth, and she ducked back into the car. "No, I didn't bring them, but I think they want me dead."

"If they wanted that, you already would be," Lucas pointed out. "They had a clean shot and didn't take it."

And it wasn't as if the men had left. Hailey could still see them on the corner of the screen. Could see the approaching cruisers, too. They pulled to a stop behind the ranch hands' truck. The doors opened, and four of Lucas's cousins—Dade, Sawyer, Josh and Gage—all took aim at the gunmen while they used the doors of the cruisers for cover.

"You're just going to let me stay out here?" Colleen protested.

Hailey was torn about what to do. Her instincts were screaming for her to protect her sister, but her instincts were even stronger to keep Camden safe.

"Answer me!" Colleen practically shouted.

"I can't let you near my son," Hailey said. "Leave and go to the sheriff's office. You'll be safe there."

That brought out some vicious profanity from Colleen. "I stopped Preston from having you killed. You owe me!"

That chilled her to the bone, but then Hailey reminded herself that it might not even be true. It could be Colleen who wanted her dead. Or even Colleen just carrying through on Preston's old wishes.

Colleen added some more profanity, but Hailey shut her out when Lucas's phone dinged, indicating he had an incoming call.

Unknown Caller popped up on the screen.

"I have to put you on hold," Lucas said to her sister, and he answered the other call.

"I know I said I'd be in touch in the morning," the man said by way of greeting, "but I just couldn't wait." It was the kidnapper, the same one who'd been communicating with them.

"Where are you?" Lucas asked.

"Nearby but out of range of all those pesky cameras you got all around the ranch. You might be able to see a couple of the fellas I brought with me, though."

"I do, and you probably see that there are six men with guns aimed right back at them."

"Yeah, they know. None of us want a gun-fight. Especially not Hailey and you. Not with your boy and all those Ryland kids and babies so close. Somebody might get hurt."

Instead of ice in Hailey's blood, that sent some hot rage through her body. How dare this snake threaten not only her son but also everyone else on the ranch? She nearly yelled at him and wanted to use some of those same curse words that her sister just had, but Lucas spoke before she could say anything.

"If you don't want a gunfight, what do you want?" Lucas asked the man.

"I thought you'd like to see who's with me," he said, obviously not answering Lucas's question. "I'm sending you a pretty picture now."

Almost immediately, Lucas's phone dinged with a text. Again from Unknown Caller, and it did indeed have a picture attached. It took a moment to load.

Hailey's heart went to her knees.

Because it was a picture of Colleen's baby. Not alone. Minton was holding her in the crook of his arm.

And there was what appeared to be a bomb strapped to Minton's chest.

Chapter Sixteen

Hailey snapped to a sitting position, and she practically snatched the phone from his hand so she could get a closer look of the photo that the kidnapper had just sent them.

But Lucas didn't need a closer look. He'd already seen more than enough.

"It could be fake," Lucas reminded Hailey. "Minton could be their boss, and he could have set all of this up."

She gave a shaky nod, repeated that last part. But he wasn't sure she was buying it. Her breathing was already way too fast, and she was no doubt having to battle the panic that had to be crawling through her. Lucas felt some of that same panic, too, but he had to rein it in so he could focus on what exactly he was seeing.

And how to fix it.

"Let me speak to Minton," Lucas told the kidnapper.

"Thought you'd want to do that. I'll put him on the line, but for just a few seconds. After that, you and I will have a little chat about what you need to do for this to turn out good for all of us."

Lucas didn't have to wait long before he heard Minton's voice. "They hit me with a stun gun when I was going into my office," Minton said, his voice a snarl. His expression in the photo matched the snarl, as well. Either he was one unhappy camper or he was pretending to be one. "Now I have a bomb on me, right next to the baby."

"Yes, I saw the photo. Is it real?" Lucas came out and asked.

"Hell, yes, it's real!" Minton's shout must have startled the baby, because she began to cry.

Not good. Hailey's nerves were clearly already frayed enough, and the baby's cries only added to the urgency of this situation.

"How do you know the bomb is real?" Lucas pressed. "Do you have personal knowledge of explosive devices?"

"Yes, I do, but not in the way you're insinuating. I didn't put this bomb on myself. These idiots did after they kidnapped me. And I don't know who they're working for, but if you don't do as they say, they're going to start the timer.

After that, I'd have only two minutes before this kid and I get blown to bits."

Lucas glanced at the photo again, at the placement of Minton's hands, and he saw that they were literally tied around the baby. Two minutes probably wouldn't be enough time to get out of those ropes and remove the bomb. Especially since it was possible the kidnappers were also holding Minton at gunpoint and wouldn't give him a chance to escape.

"Well?" the kidnapper said, coming back on the line. Lucas could still hear the baby crying, so obviously the little girl and Minton weren't too far away. "Convinced that we mean business?"

"I was convinced of that before you put an innocent baby in danger. Get the baby away from that bomb and then we'll talk."

"We'll talk now," the man snapped.

"All right," Lucas snapped right back. "You want the baby alive to collect the ransom. Well, you're risking a half million dollars by keeping her that close to the explosive."

"There's no real threat to her," the kidnapper said. "Not at this moment, anyhow. You gotta do something, though, to keep it that way. You can have the baby in exchange for Hailey. And before you go all cowboy cop on me, this isn't your decision. It's Hailey's. I'll give her five minutes to decide."

Lucas was about to tell him that he didn't need a second of that five minutes, that the answer was no. But the kidnapper hung up.

"You're not going out there," Lucas insisted.

She moved as if ready to get up, but he caught her arm to force her to sit back down. He needed to convince her to stay put, but he also had to keep watch on the security screens in case those gunmen started firing.

"These men want you dead," Lucas reminded her. "And along with two of our suspects, Colleen and Minton, there are gunmen. Going to meet them won't get the baby rescued. It will only get you killed."

She stopped struggling to get away from him, and even in the darkness, Lucas saw the tears shimmer in her eyes. "I have to do something to help that baby. She's my niece."

Lucas got that. Hell, he had a niece, and he would have done anything to keep her safe. But a suicide mission wasn't the way to go, especially since it was possible the child wasn't even in any real danger.

"So, what do we do?" Hailey asked.

He looked at the screen again. Still no movement from the gunmen. Lucas panned around, trying to get a glimpse of the vehicle holding Minton and the baby, but he didn't see anything.

Hell.

The kidnappers could have the baby anywhere, including out of the state.

"Let me see first if Colleen stayed on hold," he said.

Though Lucas wasn't sure what to tell Hailey's sister. It didn't seem a good idea to mention the bomb. However, it turned out he didn't have to make that decision, because Colleen was no longer on the line. Her car was still at the end of the road, though.

But it didn't stay there.

Colleen backed out the car, turned onto the main road and hit the accelerator. Lucas thought she had decided to leave, and he adjusted the camera angle to see if she was heading back to town.

She wasn't.

Colleen turned her car directly at the white wooden fence that fronted the ranch, and she bashed right through it. Her car went straight into the pasture. Too close to Lucas's house.

Hailey gasped. "What is she doing?" she said under her breath.

Lucas hated to think the worst, but he did. Colleen could be coming to kill them.

Dade and Gage got back into their cruiser and went in pursuit. Mason was no doubt sending someone, too, but there wasn't a lot of help to send. Most of the men were already tied up guarding the houses and the other fences, especially the back, where it would be easier for someone to launch an attack.

Colleen's car didn't make it far, though. The rain had obviously soaked the pasture, and she made it only about a hundred yards before her tires bogged down in the mud and grass. That didn't stop her, though. She barreled out of the vehicle and started running.

Directly toward Lucas's house.

He hadn't even been sure that Colleen knew which house was his, but she must have done her homework, because she was headed their way on foot.

And not alone, either.

Before Dade could get the cruiser turned around, another vehicle came up the road. A black SUV. And it looked like the same one with the attackers who'd tried to kill Hailey, Josh and him after the bombing.

"Those men are after Colleen?" Hailey asked.

Lucas didn't know the answer. Not at first, anyway. But he soon got one. The SUV didn't go after Colleen. Nor did it bog down. The driver came to a stop, and his passenger opened his door.

And the guy aimed something at Lucas's house.

It was too big to be a regular firearm, and Lucas had to zoom in on it to figure out what it was. A tear gas gun. At least, he hoped it was that and not a grenade launcher. Either way, Hailey and he had to get the heck out of there now.

Lucas closed the laptop, tucking it under his arm, and he took hold of Hailey to get her moving. It was chilly and raining, but Lucas was pretty sure there wouldn't be enough time to grab any raincoats or umbrellas.

And he was right.

There was a crashing sound of breaking glass in the living room, the side of the house that faced those thugs. Followed by another sound of the canister plinking to the floor. A couple of moments later, another canister came flying into the house.

"We have to hurry," Lucas warned her. He handed her the laptop so he could draw his gun.

Time was up, because tear gas started to spew through the entire house. Lucas ran with her to the back door and prayed he wasn't carrying Hailey right into an ambush.

HAILEY WAS MOVING as fast as she could, but it wasn't fast enough. The tear gas was on them before Lucas and she could get to the back door.

She started to cough, the gas cutting off her breath along with burning her throat and eyes. It was no doubt doing the same thing to Lucas, but he still managed to get the door open. He already had his weapon drawn when he stepped out onto the porch and looked around. He must not have seen anyone because he pulled her out of the house.

"We can't stay here," he said.

A moment later, she realized why. Another canister came bashing into the house. Then another. It wouldn't be long before the tear gas was so thick back here that they would be coughing too hard to run.

But where?

If they ran outside, they could be gunned down.

She could see Lucas's gaze darting around while he was trying to figure that out. They had a couple of choices. They could try to make it to the side of the house where he'd parked his truck. The problem with that was it was also the side where those canister-shooting thugs were positioned.

It was where she'd last seen Colleen, too.

So that probably wasn't a good direction to go. That left the barn, a detached garage and a storage building. Beyond that was open pasture, where one of those riflemen would be able to pick them off.

"We'll run to the garage," Lucas told her. "I have another truck there we can use to escape. Stay as low as you can and move fast."

Hailey wasn't sure she could go fast. Not with her legs so wobbly, and now that she couldn't breathe so well, it would be even harder. Still, they didn't have much of a choice.

Lucas took her hand and led her off the porch and down the steps. When they reached the yard, there was no more awning, so the rain and wind came right at them. Even though Hailey had on the hoodie, it wasn't nearly thick enough, and it didn't take long before she started to shiver. Still, she ran until Lucas pulled them behind a large oak.

Not a second too soon, either.

A shot blasted through the air and slammed right into the tree.

It wasn't just the rain that was raw and bitter. Suddenly the fear was, too. Not because the shot had come so close to hitting Lucas and her, but because she didn't want bullets being fired anywhere near Camden and the others.

More shots came, but these didn't slam into

the tree. That only made the fear worse because Hailey couldn't immediately figure out where those men were shooting. Then she realized they were aiming at the cruiser that Dade and Gage were trying to get closer.

Mercy.

The shooters were no doubt doing that to stop Lucas's cousins from helping them. At least the cruiser was bullet-resistant, but she figured sooner or later, either Dade or Gage would step out so they could return fire.

Hailey considered taking out the laptop to see if she could check the security cameras, but she needed to be ready to move. Plus, she didn't want to risk getting it wet. Right now, it was still under her arm where it was semiprotected. Once they were in the garage, then she could check and make sure none of these hired killers were heading for the main house. Maybe she'd also be able to find her sister. If Colleen was innocent, then she was in grave danger out in the open with those bullets flying.

Lucas's phone buzzed, and he took it from his pocket and handed it to her. Probably so he could keep his hands free. When Hailey saw Mason's name on the screen, she answered it right away.

"Is everyone all right?" she immediately asked.

"Fine for now. I want to keep it that way.

Dade told me about the bomb, the baby and Minton. As soon as Dade can, he'll move in to help. In the meantime, our other cousins, Nate and Landon, are trying to work their way to the pasture. If they get a clean shot, they'll stop the gunmen."

That was good. Hailey hoped that would happen. It wouldn't get back her niece, but it would end the immediate danger. At least, it would if these men didn't set off that explosive. But she figured they were going to use Colleen's baby as the ultimate bargaining tool to get to her.

"What about my sister?" Hailey asked. "Where is she?"

"I lost sight of her, but the last I saw her, she was moving in the direction of Lucas's barn."

Then that was all the more reason for Lucas and her not to go in there. "What about the car with Minton and the baby?"

"Still nothing on that. Grayson's coming in from town, and he'll look along the way."

Maybe they'd get lucky and could spot it. Of course, in the dark and rain, it would be hard to do.

"I can see Lucas and you," Mason went on a moment later. "Make your way to the main house when you can. You're too damn close to these dirtbags."

Yes, they were. And while Hailey desperately

wanted to see Camden, she was also terrified of having these men shoot at them if they went in that direction. Plus, Lucas and she had to get to the garage first.

"I'll have the ranch hands fire at the dirtbags," Mason added. "That should keep them occupied a couple of seconds so that you and Lucas can get moving."

"But what about the shots going to the main house?" she asked.

"The ranch hands are positioning themselves so that won't happen," he assured her.

She thanked him and added, "Just keep Camden and everyone else safe." Maybe Mason and the others would be able to do that.

She relayed the information Mason had given her to Lucas, but before she even finished, Hailey heard the shots. These weren't coming from the hired killers but rather from the ranch hands. As Mason had said, it created a distraction because the gunmen were now shooting at the hands.

"Let's move," Lucas told her.

They started running. There weren't any trees or anything else right by they could use for cover, so Hailey held her breath while they were out in the open. It seemed to take an eternity to go the fifteen or so yards. The rain certainly didn't help, either, and her shoes sank down into the boggy ground.

The moment they reached the garage, Lucas took her to the side door and threw it open. He stepped in first, his gaze slashing from one side to the other. What he didn't do was turn on the lights. Probably because it would alert the gunmen to their position. Maybe the men had been so involved with the gunfight distraction that they hadn't seen Lucas and her make their way there.

"Stay right next to me," he warned her.

She did, and while he continued to look around them, he inched his way to a truck parked at the front of the garage. The back was a workshop and storage area and was filled with shelves, tables and equipment. It would give someone places to hide. Not exactly a reminder to soothe her already raw nerves.

"I need to check and make sure no one tampered with the truck," Lucas added. "Keep watch around us."

That didn't help her nerves, either. Hailey just wanted to get out of there, but after what'd happened with the cruiser, they had to take precautions.

Lucas stooped down, and using the light from his phone, he began to make his way around the truck. She followed him while keeping watch, but Hailey didn't see anyone, thank goodness.

But she heard something.

Lucas must have, too, because he quickly stood and moved in front of her. They waited, listening. Hard to hear, though, what with the shots continuing outside, but Hailey was almost certain she'd heard something move. Or maybe it was just the wind and rain.

No, it wasn't.

There was another sound, and this time Hailey was able to pinpoint it.

Someone was in the truck.

Chapter Seventeen

Hell. What now?

Lucas pivoted and took aim in the direction of the truck cab. He didn't see anyone, but he was positive someone was in there.

He had known it was a risk to come into the garage, but it would have also been a risk for them to stay in the yard with heaven knew how many hired thugs now on the ranch. However, they might have gone from the frying pan right into the fire.

"Come out or I'll shoot," Lucas warned the person. But it was a warning he hoped like the devil that he didn't have to carry out. Because he didn't want to shoot in cramped quarters with Hailey.

Definitely didn't want to start a gunfight.

And he also didn't want to alert the armed thugs that Hailey and he were in the garage.

That would only cause them to open fire. Or maybe launch another tear gas grenade.

"It's me," someone said.

Colleen.

Lucas groaned and definitely didn't lower his gun. "Put your hands where I can see them," he ordered.

"I'm not the one trying to kill you." Colleen added a sob. "When will you believe me?"

"I might start to believe you when you get out of the truck, hands up."

Other than another sob, Colleen didn't respond, and the seconds crawled by before she finally lifted her head. Lucas could see then that she'd been down on the seat. She lifted her hands, too.

"Satisfied?" Colleen snapped.

"Not yet. Step out, keep your hands in the air and don't make any sudden moves. Get behind me," he added to Hailey. "And try to keep watch around us in case she's not alone."

Because Hailey's arm was right against his, he felt her tense even more. He hated that he was having to put her through this, but they couldn't get in the truck until Lucas figured out what the heck Colleen was up to.

Colleen stepped from the truck, and Lucas could see she didn't have anything in her hands. She also didn't appear to be carrying a weapon.

Like Hailey, Colleen wasn't wearing a coat. The rain had soaked her jeans and top, and they were clinging to her. Still, Lucas motioned for her to turn around, and when she did, he made sure she didn't have a weapon tucked in the back waist of her jeans.

She didn't.

"I told you I wasn't trying to kill you," Colleen said.

Just because she wasn't armed didn't mean she wasn't behind this attack. "Why are you in here? *How* are you in here?" Lucas amended.

"I just started running when my car got stuck. This was the first place I reached. I knew I needed to try to get to my baby, but I couldn't find the truck keys."

They were on a hook on the wall, but since Colleen hadn't turned on the lights, either, she would have had trouble spotting them.

"Do you know where the baby is?" Lucas asked.

"No." Colleen winced when there was another round of loud gunfire. "But I have to find her. I have to save her." She made a loud sob. "Is there anything you can do to make them stop shooting? Can you try to negotiate with them or something?"

Her fear seemed genuine enough, but after the hell Hailey and he had been through, Lucas planned on hanging on to his skepticism a while longer.

"I don't have any control over those gunmen," he told her. "But there are armed ranch hands out there, and they might get them to stop soon."

Colleen looked at Hailey. "Please help me get my daughter back. Please. Just think if it were your son and how hard this would be for you."

"I have thought about it," Hailey answered. "Those kidnappers want me in exchange for the baby."

"Then do it." Colleen didn't hesitate even a second, either. Maybe because she knew there was no danger for her. But there'd be plenty for Hailey. "I'd go if they would let me."

"Really?" Lucas pressed.

"Of course."

Then he was about to put that to the test. Without taking his gun off the woman, he passed his phone back to Hailey. "Hit Redial and see if the kidnapper will answer."

Colleen's eyes widened. "What are you going to do?"

Lucas didn't actually expect the kidnapper to answer and was surprised when he heard the man's voice. "Are you ready to send out Hailey?" the man asked.

"No, but Colleen is here, and she's willing to meet with you."

And Lucas carefully watched Colleen's reaction. She didn't look annoyed or afraid. "Yes," she said. "I'll come right now. Just tell me where I need to go so I can get my baby."

"Guess Lucas told you about our little explosive device, huh?" the kidnapper taunted.

Colleen's gaze slashed to Lucas. "What is he talking about?"

"So he didn't tell you," the kidnapper continued before Lucas could speak. "Minton and your baby girl are real close to a bomb right now."

Colleen gasped. "Oh, God. Is it true? Is there actually a bomb?"

"There is. A bomb set to go off with just a flip of a switch. And if you want that to change, then convince your sister to come out and chat with us. You come, too. In fact, I insist both of you come."

Even though Colleen looked on the verge of a panic attack, Lucas blocked Hailey from going closer to her. If Colleen was truly innocent, then he'd owe her a huge apology, but for now his priority had to be keeping Hailey safe.

"What exactly do you want from the women?" Lucas asked the kidnapper.

"Any and all files they have about the De-Salvo family," he answered without hesitation.

"And then what?" Hailey added.

"Then, tomorrow morning you'll get that ransom money, and you'll get both the women and the kid."

Lucas seriously doubted it. Judging from the sound she made, so did Hailey. Colleen was the only one of them who was clearly eager to do this.

"Let me know if the women are coming out," the kidnapper said. "Once they do, the shots will stop on our part. You'll have to make sure the Rylands and the ranch hands stop, too." And he ended the call.

"Call him back," Colleen insisted. "Have him tell me where Hailey and I need to go to get my baby."

"That's not going to happen," Lucas assured her. "Not on Hailey's part anyway."

But what was his next move?

He wanted to get Hailey to the main house, where she'd be safer and with Camden. However, he couldn't just leave Colleen here, either.

"Call Mason," Lucas told Hailey. "Let him know that Colleen is here, and I'm trying to figure out what to do with her. I also want to know if the road is clear between my house and his."

"You don't need to figure out what to do with me," Colleen shrieked. "We have to get the baby." She snapped toward Hailey. "This is all your fault, anyway. You probably have all sorts of information stashed away on Preston and Eric. Information that could send me to jail, too."

"Are you admitting to some crimes?" Lucas immediately asked her.

"No! But Hailey always had it in for Preston. I figure Eric, too. And if she hadn't been so hell-bent on putting them in jail, none of this would be happening."

Maybe that was true, but in this case, being hell-bent was the right thing to do. "Preston was a criminal. He deserved to be behind bars." And that was all the breath he was going to waste on Colleen. "Call Mason," he repeated to Hailey.

"I really am innocent," Colleen continued while Hailey located the number. "Darrin forced me to go to the hospital. He said it was the only way to get my baby. But he lied. And then he tried to kill me when he ran me off the road."

If that was true, then it was another reason Lucas was glad that Darrin was out of the picture. Hailey made a sound of agreement, probably because she felt the same, and she finished making the call to Mason. She also put it on speaker.

"What's the latest on the gunmen?" Lucas asked the moment his cousin answered.

"Pinned down, for now. But they're not budging, and I can't have the hands, Dade or the others go in any closer."

So they were at a stalemate. Well, in a way. Hailey was still in danger.

"Grayson called," Mason went on. "He spotted a vehicle just up the road from the ranch, and he's going to do a quiet approach to see if Minton and the baby are there. One of the deputies is with him."

"Tell the sheriff to be careful," Colleen blurted out.

"Who the hell is that?" Mason asked.

"Colleen. I'm in my garage with Hailey and her. Colleen was hiding in here."

Mason cursed. "And your plans?"

"Still debating that. How safe would it be for me to drive Hailey to the main house and then come back here to wait with Colleen?" That was just in case she was innocent and therefore in danger.

But Hailey was shaking her head before Lucas even finished his question to Mason. "That's too risky for you," she insisted.

"Hailey's right," Mason agreed. "When the gunmen spot your truck, I figure they'll start shooting at it."

Lucas wasn't giving up just yet on this particular plan. He wanted some distance between Colleen and Hailey. Between Hailey and those shooters, too. "Maybe the hands could continue keeping them occupied?"

"They could, but why don't you stay there for a couple more minutes. That'll give me time to hear from Grayson. If the baby is in that vehicle, I'll need to send him some help. Plus, I'd rather the gunmen not have any reason to get to the main house."

No way could Lucas disagree with any of that, but he definitely didn't like the idea of staying put, either. Maybe he tempted fate with that thought, because he heard a sound. Not one of the normal gunshots. This was more of a blast. One that he'd heard four other times before.

It was the sound of another gas canister being fired.

And this time it didn't smash into the house. It hit the garage door, and from what he could tell, it bashed into the wooden part of the door and not the glass inserts just above it. However, that didn't stop the gas from spewing in around the sides and bottom.

Mercy. Lucas definitely hadn't wanted things to go this way, but they had to move. That was especially true when the next canister came crashing through the glass.

"In the truck, now," he told Hailey and Colleen. He grabbed the keys from the wall hook.

They were already starting in that direction anyway. First Colleen. Then Hailey, who got in the middle. They were already coughing, too, and he hoped the tear gas didn't water his eyes so much that he wouldn't be able to see.

The moment Lucas started the engine, he hit the remote control to open the door, and once he had enough clear space to get out, he gunned the engine.

Driving right into that cloud of tear gas.

But that was just the start of their troubles. Because the gunmen started shooting at them.

HAILEY TRIED TO clear her eyes and throat so she could help Lucas get them to safety. If that was possible. The shots were coming at them so fast that it was like being trapped in a hailstorm.

The bullets tore through the windshield, and Hailey took hold of Colleen and pushed her lower on the seat. She got lower, as well, but Lucas couldn't while driving.

Lucas cursed. "Hell, they shot into the radiator."

No doubt to disable the vehicle. But how had they even known Lucas, Colleen and she were in the garage in the first place? Hailey hoped it was a guess on their part and they didn't have some insider information from Colleen. Her sister could have called or sent those thugs a text when she saw them come into the garage.

"Where are we going?" Hailey managed to ask Lucas even though she was having to fight for every breath. And she was shaking from the wet and cold. She had such a tight grip on the laptop and Lucas's phone that she was afraid they might shatter.

"Away from those shots. Away from the main house, too."

Good. As much as she wanted to get to safety, it was too risky to go in that direction. Too risky to stay put, too, and Lucas didn't speed toward the road but rather across the backyard and to the side of his own house. That put an instant buffer between them and the gunmen. What it didn't do was get rid of the lingering tear gas.

Probably because the thugs sent two more canisters their way.

The gunmen were trying to flush them out, trying to force them out into the open, where they'd be easier targets.

"Watch Colleen," Lucas said to her. A reminder that he didn't trust her sister. Neither did she, and her alarm went up a significant notch when Colleen threw open the glove compartment.

"I need a gun," her sister insisted.

Hailey wanted that, too, but she hoped there

wasn't one for Colleen to find. There wasn't. But Lucas took out his backup weapon, and when he handed it to Hailey, she had to shift the laptop under her arm so she could take it. Hailey put it in her pocket.

Giving her the gun earned Lucas and her a glare from Colleen, but Hailey didn't care. She preferred not to be in a closed vehicle with one of their armed suspects.

She lifted her head enough so she could adjust and pull out the laptop. She opened it and prayed the Wi-Fi signal was strong enough outside the house.

It was.

She pulled up the security camera screens so she could help Lucas keep watch. After all, the gunmen could sneak around the front of the house and attack. Hard to see much of anything, though, with the darkness, the tear gas and the rain, but at least the rain was washing away some of the gas. That should make it easier for them to breathe and see.

Despite the nightmare going on around them, Lucas's gaze met hers. For just a couple of seconds. She wanted to tell him how sorry she was that this had happened again.

She wanted to say a lot of things to him.

But since it wasn't the time or the place, Hailey went back to keeping watch. Right now, that was the best thing she could do for all of them. Too bad she didn't see something on the screens that would help Dade and the others close in on the gunmen. She switched the angle.

Nothing.

Then she switched it again, and that's when Hailey saw the movement. With the thick rain, it was just a blur, but someone had definitely moved up behind the two gunmen.

Another man dressed all in black. This one, though, was also wearing rain gear—a coat with a hood.

Hailey wasn't sure how he'd gotten there, but it was possible he'd come from the vehicle that had crashed through the fence. That SUV was only yards away from the other thugs.

"There's a third gunman," she relayed to Lucas.

And it made her wonder if there were others in the SUV. It tightened her stomach even more to think that there could be enough of them to overrun the ranch. Plus, there were the two across the road with the sniper rifles who had pinned down Josh and Sawyer.

"If any of the gunmen move," Lucas said, "let me know."

The words had no sooner left his mouth when the newcomer did move. He hurried behind a tree.

Coming closer to the ranch.

Closer to Lucas's house.

More movement caught her eye, and when she adjusted the camera angle, she saw the guy aim the tear gas launcher. No, not again. But he fired. Not one but two canisters.

Except these were different.

The gas coming from them was thicker, and it was milky white.

Hailey turned the laptop so that Lucas could see it, and he cursed. "Smoke bombs."

Hailey knew the reason for his profanity. As bad as the tear gas was—and it was *bad*—the smoke bombs could be worse. Because they could conceal the gunmen trying to move closer to the house.

And that's exactly what was happening.

The smoke began to spread, and it continued when the men fired off several more.

"Keep watch as best you can," Lucas advised her.

She would, but it was next to impossible to keep track of the men now. Maybe the rain, though, would work in their favor and quickly wash the smoke away as it was dissipating the tear gas.

A buzzing sound shot through the truck, and Hailey's heart jumped to her throat. At first she thought it was their attackers, but it was only

Lucas's phone. With all the chaos going on, she'd forgotten that she was still holding it.

"It's Grayson," she relayed, looking at the phone screen. She answered it right away and put it on speaker.

"Please tell me you found my baby," Colleen jumped to say.

"No, but I'm close enough to the car to see inside. There are two men in the front seat and an infant carrier in the back. The person I don't see is Minton. Any idea where he is?"

Hailey quickly scanned through all the camera angles. Even with the smoke, she could see Dade and the others pinned down. She couldn't see the gunmen, though, who'd been shooting and launching that tear gas and the smoke bombs.

But there was no sign of Minton.

"I don't know," Hailey told Grayson. "According to what the kidnapper showed us, he was in the car with the baby earlier."

"Yeah, but he's not there now, or if he is, he's down on the floor where I can't see him."

"Does that mean the bomb isn't there, either?" Colleen blurted out.

"I can't tell. But I'm going closer as soon as I have the backup that Mason's sending." Grayson paused. "Do I want to know how bad things are at the ranch?"

"The gunmen haven't gotten to the houses," Lucas answered.

What Lucas didn't say was—they hadn't, *not yet*. But there was always the possibility that they would unless the Rylands and ranch hands figured out a way to stop them.

"I'll call you back when I can," Grayson said before he hung up.

Hailey hoped he could get the baby out of there. That would be one less worry on their minds. Because even if Colleen was guilty, Hailey still wanted her niece far away from this dangerous situation.

"Where's the third gunman you saw?" Lucas asked her.

That sent Hailey's attention back to the computer screen. As she'd done before, she panned around the camera angles, looking at the tree where she'd last spotted him. But even when the smoke cleared a little in that area, there was no sign of him now.

Sweet heaven.

Because she'd gotten so preoccupied with Grayson's call, Hailey had lost sight of him. That could turn out to be a fatal mistake. Especially considering the gunman could be hiding in one of those smoke clouds that were drifting toward Lucas's house.

"Any chance the third gunman could be Minton?" Lucas added.

Hailey went back through what she'd seen of the man, but she had to shake her head. "I never saw him standing fully upright, so it's hard to know how tall he is. Plus he was wearing a hood, so I couldn't see any part of his face. But it's possible it's Minton. Or Eric."

However, it was just as likely that it was another thug who'd been hired to kill her.

"Grayson has to get to my baby," Colleen said.

Obviously she wasn't thinking about the third gunman. Maybe not even thinking about who was responsible for this. Her focus seemed to be solely on the baby. And she was crying.

Hailey was definitely affected by those tears, and it tore at her heart to think how much her sister could be suffering right now. She slid her hand over Colleen's, causing her sister to flinch. At first. Then Colleen gave her hand a gentle squeeze.

"No matter what happens," Colleen said, "I'm sorry for the way things have turned out."

Hailey was about to ask her exactly what she meant by that. But she didn't get a chance to say anything. That's because the passenger door flew open, and before Hailey could even register what was going on, someone latched onto Colleen and dragged her from the truck.

That someone put a gun to Colleen's head.

Chapter Eighteen

Lucas whipped his gun in Colleen's direction. But it was too late. The man already had her before Lucas could do anything to stop it.

However, Lucas could do something to keep Hailey safe. He crawled over her, putting himself in front of her. He didn't lower his weapon. He kept it aimed at the guy. He also watched Colleen's reaction.

She called out for help, tried to get away, but the man only jammed the gun harder against her head. It seemed convincing.

Seemed.

But Lucas reminded himself that this could all be part of the ploy to get to Hailey. A ploy he hadn't been able to prevent because he hadn't seen the guy sneaking up on the truck.

Behind him, he could hear Hailey's breath gusting, and he knew she had to be scared. Lucas hoped, though, that she would continue to keep watch around them, because heaven knew how many hired guns could be coming at them.

"Let Colleen go," Lucas demanded, though he figured this would get zero results.

And it didn't.

The guy laughed. He was wearing a tear gas mask that covered the lower part of his face, but Lucas could see enough of him to know that this wasn't Minton or Eric. He was likely just another hired gun.

"Sorry, can't let her go," the man finally said. "Got my orders, and I'm to keep this gun on her."

"Who's giving those orders?" Lucas snapped.

"It's not my place to tell, but you'll know soon enough. The boss is on the way. He should be here any minute now, and then things will get real…interesting."

Hell. Lucas had figured as much, but it was gut-tightening to hear it spelled out for him.

"Keep an eye on the security feed," Lucas told Hailey, but he wasn't even sure there was enough room for her to maneuver the laptop around so she could look. There hadn't been a lot of time when he'd moved in front of her, and she was literally jammed against him, the steering wheel and the door.

"Don't let him kill me," Colleen begged while

she stared at Lucas. "*Please.* I don't want my daughter to be an orphan."

Neither did he, but Lucas wasn't sure yet how to put a stop to this. Especially when the guy shifted the gun and took aim at him. Hailey must have seen that, because she came over his back, putting her head in front of his.

Lucas cursed at her, tried to get her to move back, but she fought him.

"He won't kill me," Hailey insisted. "Not until he's sure I've given him everything I have on the DeSalvo family. But he'll kill you."

"The little lady's right," the gunman verified. "And since I can't risk a bullet going straight through you and into her, then I have to settle for just telling you to toss out that gun."

One of the last things Lucas wanted to do was surrender his gun. But he didn't want to risk Colleen and Hailey being shot, either. So he tried to reason with this guy.

"Whatever you're getting paid, I'll double it," Lucas offered. "I can make the call now and have the funds transferred to your bank."

"That sounds real nice." The sarcasm dripped from his voice. "But doing something like that would get me killed. Besides, I'm getting paid pretty good for this. Now, throw out that gun."

Lucas felt something against his back. Hailey's hand. And it wasn't empty. She had hold of his backup weapon, no doubt a reminder that he could use that. But the problem was that once Lucas didn't have a visible weapon, this thug might change his mind about shooting.

And yes, the bullet could go through him and kill Hailey.

Even if it didn't, it could kill him, and then this thug would be able to do whatever he wanted with Colleen and Hailey.

"Time's up," the guy said without warning.

The shot blasted through the air.

Followed by Colleen's piercing scream.

Lucas felt as if someone had slugged him, and he had to fight his instincts to move away from Hailey and leave her unprotected. But it also sickened him to hear Colleen make sharp sounds of pain.

And to see the blood.

"Oh, God," Hailey said, and she would have come over Lucas if the thug hadn't pointed his weapon right at her. She stopped, freezing, but she kept repeating, "Oh, God."

"I only shot her in the arm," the man said as if that was some huge concession. Which, in a way, it was. Because he could have just as easily killed her.

The blood spread quickly across Colleen's arm, and she looked at Lucas, silently begging him to help her. He'd wanted proof that Colleen was innocent in all of this, and the gunshot was it. He seriously doubted that she would have agreed to a henchman shooting her as part of the deal.

In the distance, Lucas heard another blast from the launcher. More smoke bombs, no doubt.

"No more warnings," the gunman said to Lucas. "Toss out the gun or I shoot her again. This time I might not be so careful where I aim."

He wasn't bluffing, so Lucas had no choice but to throw his gun out of the open truck door. Now he only hoped he could get to his backup weapon when he needed it. And he would need it. He was certain of that.

"Now what?" Lucas snapped.

"We wait." The guy glanced at the back of the house, where the smoke was still the thickest. He also peeled off his gas mask. Probably because the rain had rid them of the tear gas. Lucas's eyes were still burning, but the sensation wasn't nearly as bad as it had been.

Hailey still had his phone, and Lucas heard it buzz. Mason or Grayson was probably calling. But the thug shook his head. "Let that go to voice mail."

Hailey did, and she eased the backup weapon to Lucas's side. Ideally the gunman didn't see what was going on, but he had his attention nailed to them.

"Help me," Colleen said. She was shaking now. Maybe going into shock. And she needed medical attention. However, the only way she was going to get that was for Lucas to get rid of his thug so they could call for an ambulance.

"When I move, get down," Lucas whispered to Hailey.

He felt the muscles in her body tense. Clearly, she didn't like the idea of him moving. Probably because she knew what the outcome could be. But thankfully Hailey didn't argue with him.

Lucas got ready to launch himself at the gunman. Maybe he'd be able to knock both him and his gun to the ground. Of course, Colleen would be in the middle, and Lucas prayed she didn't get hurt any worse than she already was, but if he didn't do something fast, they'd all be dead.

His phone buzzed again, distracting him for a moment. Something bad was probably going on. Maybe that bad thing didn't include Camden, but even if it did, Lucas had to put it out of his mind and try to finish this.

He didn't get far.

Lucas hadn't even started moving when he saw something out of the corner of his eye. Someone was coming toward the back of the truck. Maybe one of his brothers or a Ryland cousin.

But it wasn't.

The gunman smiled, and while he still had hold of Colleen, he moved away from the truck door, making room for their visitor.

"Told you it wouldn't be long," the gunman taunted. "The boss is here."

LUCAS SHIFTED HIS body so that it was hard for Hailey to see. He did that so he could reach the gun she was trying to give him, but it also meant she didn't know who had just arrived. She had no trouble recognizing his voice, though.

"Finally," he said.

Eric.

She hadn't known which of their suspects would be coming at them through the smoke, but Eric certainly wasn't a surprise. But was he working with Minton? Or had he come up with this all on his own?

Whatever *this* was.

"Can we leave now?" the thug asked Eric.

Eric shook his head. "Soon, though. I'm getting another vehicle up here since your idiot comrades shot out the radiator of Lucas's truck. Not very smart, and they'll pay for that."

So Eric was planning on using it to escape. But she doubted that he and his hired gum would be leaving alone. No.

Eric would try to take Colleen and her with

him, and that meant Lucas would try to stop it. He could be hurt or killed in the process.

Hailey put aside the laptop so her hands would be free in case things were about to get worse than they already were. Lucas took the gun, but there was no way he could lift it without causing Eric and the thug to shoot first. Both had their weapons aimed at Hailey and him.

"You bastard," Colleen spat out. "You took my daughter, and now you had your hired gun shoot me. And why? I erased all those files. I did everything you told me to do."

"You knew it was Eric?" Lucas asked, and he didn't sound pleased that Colleen might have withheld that from them.

Colleen shook her head. "No. But I suspected it. He knew Preston had left me money, and taking my baby was the only way to get it back."

Eric lifted his shoulder. "You didn't deserve a penny of DeSalvo money just because you slept with my father."

"I had his child!" Colleen practically shouted, but the outburst combined with the blood loss must have drained her, because she sagged against the gunman holding her. He shoved her back up, jamming the gun against her head again.

"You think that matters to me?" Eric didn't wait for her to answer. "Because it doesn't."

Hailey saw the anger rise on Eric's face and knew she couldn't let his short fuse and horrible temper come into play here. "Why did you do all of this?"

"Isn't it obvious? I don't want to die in jail like my father. You have files and information that could put me behind bars."

True, but it wasn't for anything serious.

"You made the deal with the DA," Lucas reminded him.

"It included only the recordings from my father's office." He glanced around, no doubt looking for the vehicle that was coming for them.

Lucas's phone buzzed again. The third time someone had tried to call them in the past couple of minutes. It was no doubt important. Maybe even about Camden. But Hailey didn't answer it.

"When the FBI, CSIs or some other agency with initials analyzes the voice on those tapes, they might be able to identify Melvin here." He tipped his head to the gunman. "Melvin has worked for me for years. He has a record, and it wouldn't take much to connect him to me if they were able to match his voice."

"There was no dirty agent," Lucas concluded. "But you let your father believe there was."

"You'd be surprised what I learned from the

old man when he thought he was talking to an actual agent. I made lots of money on deals where my father gave the fake guy some insider information. Of course, I had to share some of that cash with Daddy to make him think he was running things."

Yes, but Preston wouldn't have known his own son was working behind the scenes to milk him of family funds. It was all so senseless since Eric would have inherited most of it anyway.

At least, he would have, unless there'd been another child.

Oh, mercy.

"What are you going to do with your half sister?" Hailey blurted out.

That put some new alarm in Colleen's face. Probably because she'd pieced it together, as well. Eric wouldn't want any competition for the DeSalvo estate, and it was possible that the baby—and therefore Colleen—would have a claim.

"Yes," Eric said, looking at Hailey. He'd obviously seen the realization in her eyes. "And of course, you have to go, too. You know too much. Plus, I'm betting you have some dirt on me squirreled away."

Hailey was about to say that she didn't have anything else now that Colleen had deleted the files. But she changed her mind and went with something that might save them.

"If anything happens to me, the files I have will be sent to every news agency in the state," she lied.

Eric laughed, but the laughter stopped just as quickly as it'd started. "Where are the files?" he snapped. His temper was definitely showing again.

"I'm not telling you. Not until you get Colleen an ambulance and you and your hired killers are off Ryland land."

Eric's mouth tightened. "Nice try. But you're all dying. Including him." His glare slashed to Lucas. "Thanks to Hailey including you in this, she's signed your death warrant."

"Hailey didn't involve me," Lucas said, his voice low and dangerous. "*You* involved me when you tried to kill her and put my son in danger. How the hell do you possibly think you're going to get away with this?"

"Easy. I plan on pinning all of this on Minton. He's an idiot. And soon he'll be dead like the rest of you."

Sweet heaven. If Minton was anywhere near the baby, then she could be hurt, too. Or worse.

Hailey heard the sound of a car approaching from the back of the house. A moment later she saw the black SUV, the one that had brought in the gunmen. Had no doubt brought Eric, too.

"All of you will come with me," Eric insisted. "And that way I'll have some leverage to make sure Hailey gives me everything that she possibly has on me."

By leverage he meant they would become his hostages.

Eric would no doubt torture Lucas and Colleen to get Hailey to give him something she didn't have. Once he figured that out, he would indeed kill all of them. Probably Minton, too.

"Let's move," Eric said, and he used his gun to motion toward the approaching SUV.

Hailey knew that time was up. They had to do something now even though Lucas didn't have a clean shot. Eric was staying behind Colleen and his hired gun.

And Lucas did something, all right.

He sprang from the seat, barreling out of the truck, and he crashed into Colleen, Eric and the gunman.

They all went to the ground.

But the only sound Hailey heard was the shot that one of them fired.

THE SHOT WAS DEAFENING, but Lucas prayed that it hadn't hit Hailey, Colleen or him. It was hard to tell because the impact of slamming into the ground had knocked the breath out of him, and the pain spiked through him when his jaw collided with the hired gun's Glock.

Lucas hadn't wanted things to play out this way, but Eric hadn't given him much of a choice. If they'd gotten into that SUV with him and his hired killers, Colleen, Hailey and he would have soon been dead.

Colleen screamed when they fell, but Lucas still didn't know if she'd been shot again. That's because the fight started almost immediately. The thug slammed his gun against Lucas's head so hard that it probably gave him a concussion.

That didn't stop Lucas from fighting, though. The stakes were too high for him to lose. He still had hold of his gun, but it was too risky to get a shot off now. He had to get Colleen out of the way first, and that wouldn't be easy since she was trapped between Eric and him.

Eric spewed out a string of profanity, and for a guy who didn't work with his hands, he was fighting hard. He was also trying to shoot Lucas. Eric brought up his gun, but Lucas managed to knock it away in the nick of time.

Eric's shot blasted into the ground right next to Lucas.

Hailey yelled out something. Something that Lucas didn't catch, but he hoped she would stay back.

She didn't.

He saw her out of the corner of his eye. She had gotten out of the truck and had picked up his gun. The one he'd thrown out of the truck. She was trying to take aim, but there was no way she'd have a clean shot.

But Eric did.

The goon was punching Lucas, but he still managed to see Eric lift his gun again. And this time he aimed it at Hailey.

"Get down!" Lucas shouted to her.

He wasn't sure if she did—not in time, anyway—before Eric pulled the trigger again. Lucas didn't look to see where the shot had gone. Instead he shifted his weight, shoving Colleen out of the way so that he could pin down Eric.

Melvin was obviously looking out for his boss, because he walloped Lucas in the head again. More than anything, Lucas wanted to shoot the guy, but he couldn't let go of Eric to do that.

Someone fired, though.

Hailey.

She'd shot into the ground. Maybe to distract Eric and Melvin. If so, it worked in a bad way. Melvin looked at Hailey.

And he took aim.

That meant Lucas had to release Eric so he

could dive at Melvin. Melvin still managed to pull the trigger, but Lucas was able to throw Melvin enough off balance that he didn't shoot Hailey. But Melvin had come darn close to doing just that.

Too close.

Lucas couldn't tell her that now because he was fighting for their lives, but later he wanted her to know that she should never take a risk like that again. Because she could have been killed. He could have lost her.

Colleen scurried away from them, and while she was holding her injured arm, she ran to Hailey. Maybe because Hailey didn't see it coming, Colleen wrenched the gun from her hand. Colleen pointed it at the men.

"Give me back my daughter, Eric," Colleen shouted. "Or so help me, I'll kill you right now."

Lucas prayed she didn't shoot, because the way she was shaking, there was no telling who Colleen might hit. His cousins were likely nearby, and a stray shot could kill one of them. It also caused his heart to slam against his chest when he saw that Hailey was trying to get the gun back from her sister. No way did he want Hailey in a struggle—any kind of struggle— where there was a gun involved.

Since every second this went on was another second when someone could get killed,

Lucas threw his own gun aside so he could latch onto Melvin's. Of course, Eric took full advantage of that. He tried to take aim again, but Lucas stopped him by slamming his elbow into Eric's jaw. Eric howled in pain and dropped back down to the ground.

A shot cracked through the air.

Lucas's breath stopped, and despite being in a fistfight with Melvin, he glanced at Hailey to make sure she was all right. She wasn't. She was seemingly frozen with both Colleen's and her hands on the gun.

Melvin cursed, and he froze as well.

Lucas looked on the ground beside him and saw Eric. Bleeding. The shot that Colleen had fired had hit him in the stomach.

"You're gonna pay for that!" Melvin yelled, and he tried to turn his gun on Colleen.

Lucas didn't let that happen. He used the new surge of adrenaline that he got to grab Melvin's gun. Of course, Melvin didn't just give it up. He kept trying to aim it at Colleen. But instead, Lucas turned the gun on the hired killer.

Just as Melvin pulled the trigger.

The bullet went into his chest. Since the shot was at point-blank range, Melvin didn't even draw another breath. It killed him instantly.

Lucas didn't waste a second on the gunman. Instead, he took the guy's weapon and aimed it at Eric. He also kicked Eric's gun from his hand and took aim at him in case he tried to move. He did, but it was only to clutch his stomach and his chest.

And he laughed.

"You think this is over," Eric said, looking at Colleen and Hailey. "It's not."

That's when Lucas realized that Eric wasn't just holding his hand to his gunshot wound. He pressed something on his chest. A small box that resembled a remote control on a garage.

A split second later, Lucas heard a sound he definitely didn't want to hear.

An explosion.

Chapter Nineteen

"No!" Colleen yelled.

Lucas didn't yell, but he frantically looked around to see if he could find the source of the explosion. It hadn't come from the area where the tear gas had been launched. No. This was further away. Just up the road from the ranch.

In the same area where Grayson had said he'd spotted the kidnapper's vehicle.

Colleen must have realized that, too, because despite her injury, she turned and started to run in that direction.

"Stop her," Lucas told Hailey. Though he hated to give an order like that since Colleen was still armed. It was obvious she was hysterical, and there was no telling what she might do.

Lucas checked first to make sure there were no weapons near Eric. He was bleeding, maybe dying, but that didn't mean he wouldn't be able to shoot them. It would be the ultimate way to get his revenge.

Hailey hooked her arm around Colleen's waist but didn't have a solid enough footing and her sister slung her to the ground. That meant a change of plan. Lucas scooped up one of the guns and handed it to Hailey.

"Make sure Eric doesn't get up," he told her, and he took off running after Colleen. There were possibly some of Eric's hired guns still in the area, and he didn't want Colleen shot for a second time tonight. The next bullet just might kill her.

Might kill him, too.

Lucas only hoped they didn't get caught in the middle of a gunfight.

He had to tackle Colleen, dragging them both to the ground again. This couldn't be good for her injury since she was still bleeding. But despite that injury, she fought like a wildcat.

"I have to get to my baby!" she shouted.

Yeah, Lucas understood that, but he shook his head and got in her face. "You can't go down there. It's a good quarter of a mile away, and you'll be killed."

Logic wasn't going to work here, so he just pinned her to the ground with his body and wrenched the gun from her hand. Colleen kept fighting him, punching his chest with her fists, and Lucas just let her do it while he kept watch to make sure they weren't about to be ambushed.

He looked back at Hailey. Even from a distance he could see that she was shaking, but she still had the gun aimed at Eric. Eric wasn't saying anything, wasn't moving, either. Lucas had rarely wished someone dead, but he hoped in this case that Eric was so that he would no longer be a threat to Hailey and Colleen.

But there were other threats out there.

Colleen finally quit fighting, her hands dropping to the ground, and she sobbed. The tears came, mixed with the rain on her face, but Lucas could deal with the tears as long as she didn't run out into the path of those possible gunmen. Now that he knew Colleen was innocent in all of this, he definitely wanted to make sure he kept Hailey's sister alive.

He got up, pulling Colleen to her feet, and he took her to the truck, pushing her into the middle so Hailey could get in, as well. He wouldn't be able to drive the truck, but at least being inside it was better than having them stay in the open.

Hailey had such a fierce grip on the gun and her muscles were so rigid that it took Lucas a moment to get her moving. When he finally did, she sagged against him.

"The baby," she said.

Lucas figured she was praying that her niece was okay. He was doing the same and adding some extra prayers for Camden and the rest of his family.

"Both of you stay down," Lucas told them once he had Hailey in the cab of the truck.

She nodded, took out his phone and showed him the screen with the missed calls. All three were from Mason. Lucas certainly hadn't forgotten about them, but he wanted to keep his hands, and his attention, free in case they were attacked again.

Hailey must have understood that, because she hit the redial button and put it on speaker. Mason answered on the first ring.

"What the hell was that explosion?" Mason immediately asked.

"I'm not sure." Lucas didn't want to spell out his worst fears. "Have you talked to Grayson?"

"He's not answering his phone, and he's nowhere near any of the security cameras. Please tell me he wasn't near that bomb when it went off."

Lucas didn't know, and again he didn't want to guess. Grayson was smart, so maybe he'd made it out of there with the baby.

"The reason I called you earlier was to warn

you about Eric," Mason went on. "I saw him on one of the cameras. Is he dead?"

"Not yet. Can you call an ambulance for Colleen and him?" Lucas asked.

"Already done, and they're on the way. Dade and the others have cleared the gunmen so the medics can get through. I'll send a cruiser down to pick up Colleen, Hailey and you. Colleen is innocent, right?"

Lucas glanced back at her. "Yeah." Innocent and shaken to the core. Also still losing some blood. Hailey had peeled off her hoodie and was using it as a makeshift tourniquet.

"Good," Mason answered. "Then the three of you can come here. I'll have Dade or someone wait with Eric. Let me know the moment you hear anything from Grayson."

"I will." Lucas looked around the yard again. "Are you sure the gunmen are all out of commission?"

"All the ones on the ranch grounds. The ones across the road, too." He paused. "Don't know about Minton, though."

Yes. Lucas hadn't forgotten about him, either. Eric had claimed there was no dirty agent, and that should clear Minton's name. If Eric was telling the truth.

Lucas heard the sound of an approaching car coming from the main part of the ranch, and he automatically pivoted in that direction with his gun aimed and ready. But it wasn't one of Eric's thugs. It was Sawyer and Josh. Josh hurried out of the cruiser toward them.

"I drew the short straw," Josh said. "Go ahead with Sawyer. I'll make sure Eric doesn't go anywhere."

Lucas hated to put this on his cousin, but one look at Hailey and Colleen and he knew he had to get them out of there. He thanked Josh, and because he didn't want the women out in the open any longer than necessary, he scooped up Colleen and took her to the cruiser. He would have gone back and done the same for Hailey, but she was already trailing along behind him. He put Colleen in the front seat. Hailey and he took the back.

"I'm okay," Hailey said to him.

It was almost certainly a lie, but Lucas latched onto it. He also latched onto her. He pulled her into his arms, probably with a lot harder grip than either of them had been expecting.

The relief came. She was alive and in one piece. No thanks to Eric. That fight could have played out a dozen different ways, and in any one of the scenarios, Hailey could have been hurt or worse.

Colleen, however, wasn't faring as well. She was sobbing now, hunched over and probably in a lot of pain. Maybe it wouldn't be long before the ambulance arrived, though Lucas was worried that she might not go to the hospital until they got news about the baby.

It wasn't a long trip to the main house, but it certainly felt like one. Lucas kept watch the whole way, but thankfully he didn't see any signs of danger.

Only the aftermath.

He spotted one of the gunmen, dead, in the pasture. Not far from where they'd launched the smoke bombs and the tear gas. The goon and his fellow hired thugs had turned the Silver Creek Ranch into a war zone. That twisted at Lucas's gut. But it was also something he had to push aside.

For Hailey's sake.

Heck, for his own peace of mind.

Because he thought they could both use it, he brushed a kiss on Hailey's forehead. Then her cheek. Yes, they both needed that. Needed the real kiss that followed, too. It wasn't nearly long enough, but Lucas figured he could do better later. Later, he wanted to do a lot of things. Like tell Hailey that he had died a thousand times tonight worrying about her, and that it had driven home to him just how important she was to him.

"I'm in love with you," Hailey blurted out.

Judging from the startled look in her eyes,

she hadn't intended to say that. Nor did she have time to add more, because Sawyer pulled to a stop directly in front of the main house, and that was their cue to get moving. Sawyer helped with Colleen, but before they even made it up the steps, Lucas heard two welcome sounds.

The ambulance sirens.

And his son.

Camden was fussing, and while it was obvious he wasn't happy about something, just hearing him eased the knot in Lucas's stomach.

Despite her limp, Hailey hurried in ahead of them. And Lucas let her. She looked around the massive foyer. No sign of Camden there, but he was in the adjacent family room with Tillie and Mason's wife, Abbie. Tillie was pacing while rocking Camden, obviously trying to get him to sleep. Hailey went to him and pulled him into her arms.

Camden stopped fussing right away and studied her face. Hailey was still pretty much a stranger to him, but that didn't stop his boy from smiling. He smiled even more when he looked in Lucas's direction.

Everything suddenly seemed all right with the world.

Well, almost everything. His phone buzzed, and when he saw Grayson's name on the screen, Lucas knew this was a call he had to take.

"Is it about the baby?" Colleen asked. Sawyer was trying to get her to sit, but she batted away his hands and went to Lucas.

Lucas figured it was indeed about the baby, but he wasn't sure it would be good news. No way to buffer it from Colleen, though, since she was right next to him. Because she would probably be able to hear every word anyway, he went ahead and put it on speaker.

"I have the baby," Grayson immediately said.

Lucas could feel the relief go through the room, and Hailey went to her sister to give her a hug. Colleen broke down again, crying, but Lucas figured these were happy tears.

"Is she okay? Was she hurt?" Colleen blurted out.

"She's fine," Grayson answered. "I'm bringing her to the ranch right now. The ambulance is ahead of me."

Which meant Colleen wouldn't have much time with her daughter before being whisked away to the hospital. She wouldn't care much for that, but Colleen needed medical attention ASAP. She also clearly needed to see her daughter right away, because she started toward the door and would have hurried out, no doubt to watch for Grayson. But Lucas stopped her. He didn't want any one of them outside just yet.

"What about the explosion?" Hailey asked.

"The bomb detonated after the baby was already out of the car," Grayson answered. "Minton killed the kidnapper, but he couldn't disarm the bomb, so he took the baby and ran. When I'd looked in the SUV earlier with the binoculars, I thought she was still in the vehicle, but it was only her car seat that I saw."

Good. Lucas hated that the baby had even had to go through a nightmare like that, but at least she wasn't near the blast.

Thanks to Minton.

"Where is Minton?" Lucas pressed.

"With me."

Lucas felt no regret about that whatsoever and hoped all of Eric's hired thugs were dead or arrested. And speaking of Eric, he needed to give Grayson an update on the idiot who'd done his best to make their lives a living hell.

"Minton won't be staying," Grayson continued. "He wants to borrow a vehicle to get him back to his office, so once I'm at the house, I'll let him use my truck."

Even though Minton was innocent and had helped them by saving the baby, Lucas could understand why the agent didn't want to hang around. He hadn't exactly been friendly to Hailey and the rest of them. Plus, like Grayson, he probably had reports to write up about the attack.

"If Eric's still alive, he'll need to go to the hospital, too," Lucas said.

"Yeah. I got a call from Dade. Eric died a couple of minutes ago. The ME will come out and take care of the body. The bodies of the other gunmen, as well."

Lucas thanked him. He definitely didn't want any of his cousins or their families waking up to a giant crime scene, so maybe the bodies and the debris could be cleared out by morning.

Grayson had been right about the ambulance, because Lucas heard the siren as it made the turn toward the main house. He wished he could talk Hailey into going to the hospital, too, to be checked out, but judging from the grip she had on Camden, that wasn't going to happen.

"Maybe I can ride with the baby and Colleen in the ambulance?" Tillie suggested. Lucas wanted to kiss the woman for making the offer. "Unless Hailey and you need me here for Camden, that is."

"No," Hailey and Lucas said in unison. They'd be just fine now that the danger had passed.

Well, maybe it had passed.

"Are we sure there are no more hired killers?" Lucas asked Grayson.

"The hands and deputies are doing a final search now, but there's no one shooting. Just in case one's hiding, Sawyer and Josh are going to do a sweep with infrared. Mason's still in his office checking the security cameras."

Hailey closed her eyes a moment, nodded. She was obviously thankful for these extra security measures. It would help everyone get some sleep for what was left of the night. Everyone except Colleen. But he figured she wouldn't mind. She was alive, and her baby had been rescued.

Grayson ended the call just as the ambulance pulled to a stop in front of the house, and this time Lucas wasn't able to hold Colleen back. That's because Grayson had said he was right behind the medics. And he was. He didn't waste any time getting out and bringing the baby to Colleen.

There were more tears, of course, and Colleen hugged her daughter as tightly as Hailey was hugging Camden.

"You should go," Grayson prompted Colleen. Apparently he'd already given his keys to Minton, because the agent drove away.

Colleen managed a shaky nod, but despite the fact she was bleeding, she carried the baby toward the ambulance. Tillie was right behind her.

"Call me when you can," Hailey told her sister. "And if the doctors keep you at the hospital overnight, I'll be there first thing in the morning."

Despite everything that had gone on, Colleen managed a weak smile and a thank-you. Maybe this was the start of a better relationship between the sisters.

"Tell Mason I'm taking his cruiser," Grayson said to Abbie. "If anyone needs me, I'll be with the ME and then at the office."

Lucas felt guilty since Grayson had a long stretch of work ahead of him. And he'd help. But not tonight. Tonight he needed to be with Hailey and Camden.

"Do you want me to take Camden?" Abbie asked.

Lucas certainly hadn't forgotten about Mason's wife being there, but he didn't understand her question. No way did he want Camden out of his sight. But Lucas looked at Hailey. Then himself. They were soaking wet, covered in mud, blood and heaven knew what else.

"You can use the showers in the guest rooms," Abbie suggested.

"In just a couple of minutes." Hailey kissed Camden's cheek, and despite the fact that he was right up against her wet clothes, he didn't seem to mind.

Abbie must have decided they needed some alone time, because she disappeared down the hall. Probably to check on her own sons.

Hailey got a few more kisses and then passed Camden to Lucas so he could do the same. It was pure magic. Somehow, just holding his son could melt away most of the misery from the past couple of days.

But misery wasn't the only thing that'd happened tonight.

"You said you were in love with me," Lucas reminded Hailey.

She made a soft sound of surprise. "Yes, *that*." Then she dodged his gaze and opened her mouth to say something that Lucas realized he might not want to hear.

"You can't take it back," he growled, and then frowned when he heard the tone of his own voice. He hadn't meant to make it sound like an order. "Please don't take it back," he amended.

Hailey didn't make another sound of surprise, but judging from the way her eyes widened, she certainly hadn't been expecting that from him. Well, Lucas hadn't expected it, either. Nor was he sure when he'd wanted Hailey's "I'm in love with you," but he definitely wanted it.

With Camden in the crook of his left arm, Lucas slid his right hand around Hailey's waist and pulled her closer. He kissed her. Not some gentle, everything-will-be-all-right kind of kiss, either. This was long and deep. Just the way he liked his kisses when it came to Hailey.

The kiss stirred the heat between them, but it did more than that. It made things crystal clear for Lucas.

"I fell in love with you shortly after we met," he said with his lips still against hers. "That hasn't changed. Never will. I want you in my bed…my life. Our lives," he added, glancing down at Camden.

And Lucas pulled back so he could see her reaction. He expected her to be stunned. Maybe even have a run-for-the-hills kind of look in her eyes.

She didn't.

Hailey smiled, slow and easy. A smile that lit up her whole face, and she pulled him right back to her for another kiss. "Good. And you can't take it back."

Lucas had no intentions of ever taking it back. Ever. He gathered Hailey and his son into his arms and held on.

* * * * *

*There's much more to come from
Delores Fossen in 2017.
Don't miss BRANDED AS TROUBLE
on sale in July from HQN Books.*

And in the fall, this USA TODAY
*bestselling author launches a
brand-new miniseries in
Harlequin Intrigue!*

Get 2 Free Books,
Plus 2 Free Gifts —

HARLEQUIN *Presents*

just for trying the Reader Service!

YES! Please send me 2 FREE Harlequin Presents® novels and my 2 FREE gifts (gifts are worth about $10 retail). After receiving them, if I don't wish to receive any more books, I can return the shipping statement marked "cancel." If I don't cancel, I will receive 6 brand-new novels every month and be billed just $4.55 each for the regular-print edition or $5.55 each for the larger-print edition in the U.S., or $5.49 each for the regular-print edition or $5.99 each for the larger-print edition in Canada. That's a saving of at least 11% off the cover price! It's quite a bargain! Shipping and handling is just 50¢ per book in the U.S. and 75¢ per book in Canada.* I understand that accepting the 2 free books and gifts places me under no obligation to buy anything. I can always return a shipment and cancel at any time. Even if I never buy another book, the 2 free books and gifts are mine to keep forever.

Please check one: ☐ Harlequin Presents® Regular-Print   ☐ Harlequin Presents® Larger-Print
(106/306 HDN GLP6)   (176/376 HDN GLP7)

Name _____ (PLEASE PRINT)

Address _____ Apt. # _____

City _____ State/Prov. _____ Zip/Postal Code _____

Signature (if under 18, a parent or guardian must sign)

Mail to the **Reader Service:**
IN U.S.A.: P.O. Box 1867, Buffalo, NY 14240-1867
IN CANADA: P.O. Box 611, Fort Erie, Ontario L2A 9Z9

Want to try two free books from another series? Call 1-800-873-8635 or visit www.ReaderService.com.

* Terms and prices subject to change without notice. Prices do not include applicable taxes. Sales tax applicable in N.Y. Canadian residents will be charged applicable taxes. Offer not valid in Quebec. This offer is limited to one order per household. Books received may not be as shown. Not valid for current subscribers to Harlequin Presents books. All orders subject to credit approval. Credit or debit balances in a customer's account(s) may be offset by any other outstanding balance owed by or to the customer. Please allow 4 to 6 weeks for delivery. Offer available while quantities last.

Your Privacy—The Reader Service is committed to protecting your privacy. Our Privacy Policy is available online at www.ReaderService.com or upon request from the Reader Service.

We make a portion of our mailing list available to reputable third parties that offer products we believe may interest you. If you prefer that we not exchange your name with third parties, or if you wish to clarify or modify your communication preferences, please visit us at www.ReaderService.com/consumerchoice or write to us at Reader Service Preference Service, P.O. Box 9062, Buffalo, NY 14240-9062. Include your complete name and address.

HP17R

Get 2 Free Books,
Plus 2 Free Gifts—
just for trying the Reader Service!

YES! Please send me 2 FREE LARGER PRINT Harlequin® Romance novels and my 2 FREE gifts (gifts are worth about $10 retail). After receiving them, if I don't wish to receive any more books, I can return the shipping statement marked "cancel." If I don't cancel, I will receive 4 brand-new novels every month and be billed just $5.34 per book in the U.S. or $5.74 per book in Canada. That's a savings of at least 15% off the cover price! It's quite a bargain! Shipping and handling is just 50¢ per book in the U.S. and 75¢ per book in Canada.* I understand that accepting the 2 free books and gifts places me under no obligation to buy anything. I can always return a shipment and cancel at any time. Even if I never buy another book, the two free books and gifts are mine to keep forever.

119/319 HDN GLPW

Name _____ (PLEASE PRINT)

Address _____ Apt. #

City _____ State/Prov. _____ Zip/Postal Code

Signature (if under 18, a parent or guardian must sign)

Mail to the **Reader Service:**

IN U.S.A.: P.O. Box 1867, Buffalo, NY 14240-1867
IN CANADA: P.O. Box 611, Fort Erie, Ontario L2A 9Z9
Want to try two free books from another line?
Call 1-800-873-8635 or visit www.ReaderService.com.

* Terms and prices subject to change without notice. Prices do not include applicable taxes. Sales tax applicable in N.Y. Canadian residents will be charged applicable taxes. Offer not valid in Quebec. This offer is limited to one order per household. Books received may not be as shown. Not valid for current subscribers to Harlequin Romance Larger Print books. All orders subject to credit approval. Credit or debit balances in a customer's account(s) may be offset by any other outstanding balance owed by or to the customer. Please allow 4 to 6 weeks for delivery. Offer available while quantities last.

Your Privacy—The Reader Service is committed to protecting your privacy. Our Privacy Policy is available online at www.ReaderService.com or upon request from the Reader Service.

We make a portion of our mailing list available to reputable third parties that offer products we believe may interest you. If you prefer that we not exchange your name with third parties, or if you wish to clarify or modify your communication preferences, please visit us at www.ReaderService.com/consumerschoice or write to us at Reader Service Preference Service, P.O. Box 9062, Buffalo, NY 14240-9062. Include your complete name and address.

HRLP17R

Get 2 Free Books,
<u>Plus</u> 2 Free Gifts —
just for trying the
Reader Service!

HARLEQUIN *Superromance*

YES! Please send me 2 FREE LARGER-PRINT Harlequin® Superromance® novels and my 2 FREE gifts (gifts are worth about $10 retail). After receiving them, if I don't wish to receive any more books, I can return the shipping statement marked "cancel." If I don't cancel, I will receive 4 brand-new novels every month and be billed just $6.19 per book in the U.S. or $6.49 per book in Canada. That's a savings of at least 11% off the cover price! It's quite a bargain! Shipping and handling is just 50¢ per book in the U.S. or 75¢ per book in Canada.* I understand that accepting the 2 free books and gifts places me under no obligation to buy anything. I can always return a shipment and cancel at any time. Even if I never buy another book, the 2 free books and gifts are mine to keep forever.

132/332 HDN GLQN

Name	(PLEASE PRINT)	
Address		Apt. #
City	State/Prov.	Zip/Postal Code

Signature (if under 18, a parent or guardian must sign)

Mail to the **Reader Service:**
IN U.S.A.: P.O. Box 1867, Buffalo, NY 14240-1867
IN CANADA: P.O. Box 611, Fort Erie, Ontario L2A 9Z9

Want to try two free books from another line?
Call 1-800-873-8635 today or visit www.ReaderService.com.

* Terms and prices subject to change without notice. Prices do not include applicable taxes. Sales tax applicable in N.Y. Canadian residents will be charged applicable taxes. Offer not valid in Quebec. This offer is limited to one order per household. Books received may not be as shown. Not valid for current subscribers to Harlequin Superromance Larger-Print books. All orders subject to credit approval. Credit or debit balances in a customer's account(s) may be offset by any other outstanding balance owed by or to the customer. Please allow 4 to 6 weeks for delivery. Offer available while quantities last.

Your Privacy—The Reader Service is committed to protecting your privacy. Our Privacy Policy is available online at www.ReaderService.com or upon request from the Reader Service.

We make a portion of our mailing list available to reputable third parties that offer products we believe may interest you. If you prefer that we not exchange your name with third parties, or if you wish to clarify or modify your communication preferences, please visit us at www.ReaderService.com/consumerchoice or write to us at Reader Service Preference Service, P.O. Box 9062, Buffalo, NY 14240-9062. Include your complete name and address.

HSRLP17

HOMETOWN HEARTS ♡

YES! Please send me **The Hometown Hearts Collection** in Larger Print. This collection begins with 3 FREE books and 2 FREE gifts in the first shipment. Along with my 3 free books, I'll also get the next 4 books from the Hometown Hearts Collection, in LARGER PRINT, which I may either return and owe nothing, or keep for the low price of $4.99 U.S./ $5.89 CDN each plus $2.99 for shipping and handling per shipment*. If I decide to continue, about once a month for 8 months I will get 6 or 7 more books, but will only need to pay for 4. That means 2 or 3 books in every shipment will be FREE! If I decide to keep the entire collection, I'll have paid for only 32 books because 19 books are FREE! I understand that accepting the 3 free books and gifts places me under no obligation to buy anything. I can always return a shipment and cancel at any time. My free books and gifts are mine to keep no matter what I decide.

262 HCN 3432 462 HCN 3432

Name	(PLEASE PRINT)	
Address		Apt. #
City	State/Prov.	Zip/Postal Code

Signature (if under 18, a parent or guardian must sign)

Mail to the **Reader Service:**
IN U.S.A.: P.O. Box 1867, Buffalo, NY. 14240-1867
IN CANADA: P.O. Box 609, Fort Erie, Ontario L2A 5X3

* Terms and prices subject to change without notice. Prices do not include applicable taxes. Sales tax applicable in NY. Canadian residents will be charged applicable taxes. This offer is limited to one order per household. All orders subject to approval. Credit or debit balances in a customer's account(s) may be offset by any other outstanding balance owed by or to the customer. Please allow 4 to 6 weeks for delivery. Offer available while quantities last. Offer not available to Quebec residents.

Your Privacy—The Reader Service is committed to protecting your privacy. Our Privacy Policy is available online at www.ReaderService.com or upon request from the Reader Service.

We make a portion of our mailing list available to reputable third parties that offer products we believe may interest you. If you prefer that we not exchange your name with third parties, or if you wish to clarify or modify your communication preferences, please visit us at www.ReaderService.com/consumerchoice or write to us at Reader Service Preference Service, P.O. Box 9062, Buffalo, NY. 14240-9062. Include your complete name and address.

HHBPA17